FALL INTO MAGIC

Seasons of Summer Novella Series: Book One

_____

MELISSA BALDWIN

Copyright © 2016 Melissa Baldwin

ISBN: 0692785299
ISBN 13: 978-0692785294

Formatted by Karan & Co. Author Solutions

About Fall Into Magic

After enduring a devastating breakup in the middle of my summer vacation, I, Summer Peters, know I need a distraction. Thankfully I have the arrival of fall, Halloween, and a new client to keep me occupied. I assume that successful Alexander Williams will be a hands-off client, and I especially don't expect him to be so down-to-earth. I'm immediately drawn to him, much to the dismay of his overprotective assistant. When it becomes obvious that he feels the same, I begin to wonder if our meeting was fate.

With my life heading in the right direction, I begin the process of moving on—until my ex-boyfriend Jake returns begging for a second chance. And, imagine my surprise to learn my nosy, meddling neighbor is a psychic who's threatening to reveal details of my future.

I hate feeling like I'm being pulled in different directions. Between Alexander, his assistant, and my ex-boyfriend, I fear I may not be ready to move on after all. I could always turn to my neighbor for advice, but the fear of hearing exactly what the future holds is more frightening than not knowing.

Join Summer on a wild one-year journey in the of the Seasons of Summer Series from USA Today bestselling author Melissa Baldwin

I dedicate this book to my miracle baby girl who shares my love of all things fall and Halloween.

Chapter One

I look out over the crashing waves as I enjoy my last few hours of vacation. Why do these hours always go by so quickly? I'm trying to soak up every last second, even though this summer coming to an end is somewhat bittersweet for me.

What should have been one of the best summers of my life definitely changed a few weeks ago when my boyfriend, Jake—insert: now ex-boyfriend—decided to end things. Who ends things in the middle of a fantastic vacation anyway? I could go into detail about his explanation, but I'd rather not relive those horrible fifteen minutes again. And to be honest, his explanation was rather vague. Let's just say "I'm not sure I'm ready to be in such a serious relationship" came into play. It was bad enough having to explain to my friends why Jake decided to head back to Connecticut early. My friend Angie's aunt has a place at Gurney's Inn and we've enjoyed summers here for several years. This is by far the worst one, at least for me.

Anyway, it took Jake all of fifteen minutes to wrap up an amazing eighteen months together. Following his quick breakup, I spent several hours doing the usual things women do after being dumped. I cried as I poured over photos and listened to sad love songs. And my friend Angie bought me three boxes of Little Debbie Swiss Cake Rolls, which I devoured over the following two days.

As devastating as it has been, there is light at the end of the tunnel and I'm trying my hardest to focus on that light. Fall is around the corner and that gives me something to concentrate on and look forward to. At least I still have my job, and first thing on Monday morning, I begin work with a new client, which will give me an opportunity to immerse myself into someone else's home (i.e. life). Thankfully, I'm one of those people who enjoys my career as an interior decorator. So, as sad as it is watching the summer roll away with the waves, I'm ready to begin the next new chapter in my life . . . I think.

"Are you thinking about Jake?" Angie asks as she sits down and crosses her legs on the lounge chair next to me. She rips open a package of Chocolate Twizzlers, holding it out to me. Typical Angie, she eats more junk food than anyone I've ever met but you would never know it. She's a marathon runner so that definitely helps to balance out her love of all things sweet and fattening. I take three pieces because—well, you know, when in Rome.

"No I'm not," I lie. "Well, not entirely."

She sighs as she looks out over the ocean. "Another summer comes to an end."

I nod. "That's actually what I was thinking about." I pause. "It's okay, though. I'm ready to get back. I have plenty of work to keep me busy."

She chews on a piece of Twizzlers. "Did Jake already pick up his stuff?"

I roll my eyes. "Yep. He texted to tell me that he left his key with nosy Mrs. Rothera, who lives downstairs. Now I'm going to have to give her an explanation, too, because you know how she lives for all the gossip."

"At least your dad will be happy," she adds. That is true; my dad never liked Jake, so this is sure to please him. He never told me why he didn't like him, though. He would just say that he had a feeling about him. Looking back, I really wish he would have told me why. He could have saved me several months of my life and definitely some tears. It's probably something silly like him being a Giants fan instead of a Jets fan. Football is a huge deal in my family being that my father has been a coach for years. I guess I should have known better from day one.

"Yes, he will," I agree. "But I'm not ready to admit he was right just yet. Still, I told Jake I would get the key from him later but he clearly wanted to be free of all ties to me."

"Oh well, it's his loss. He couldn't face you, what a loser," Angie shouts. Angie is so loud, being born and raised in Staten Island and coming from a big Italian family will do that to you. I do appreciate her loyalty, though—she's been my rock these past few weeks.

"Are you ready to get back?" I ask. She shrugs her shoulders. "I guess all good things come to an end."

I give her a sad smile. "Yes, they do."

Home sweet home. As soon as I walk into my apartment I look around to see if Jake left anything—of course, he didn't. He really couldn't wait to get the hell out of here. We actually didn't live together but he was here all the time being that he has a roommate. Oh well, it's his loss just like Angie said. I need to make myself busy so I don't get sad again.

As much as I love traveling, I really hate this part—the unpacking and laundry is worse than a trip to the dentist. After I throw a load in the washer, I make myself a cup of peppermint tea and open my laptop. Time to get in work mode. I look over the proposal I put together for my new client, Alexander Williams. I haven't had the opportunity to meet Alexander yet, but I did do what every normal person in the world would—I stalked his social media. I admit I almost fell off my barstool when I first searched him out—a) he looks like Clark Kent from *Superman*, and b) his favorite movie is *Grease 2*, which also happens to be my favorite movie. Not that it's a big deal for him to like the movie, but it definitely caught my eye when he posted that he was watching *Grease 2* and always dreamed of being a T-Bird. I'm sure he only cares about watching Michelle Pfeiffer, and to give credit where credit is due, she was stunning in that movie. When I was younger, I wished I looked like Michelle Pfeiffer with her blonde locks and blue eyes. My mom would always get mad when I said this; she told me to embrace my brown eyes and thick reddish-brown hair. Don't get me wrong, I do love my hair and so does everyone else, but I think it's pretty normal to want what we can't have. I must get at least ten compliments a day on my hair . . . Jake always loved my hair. Crap, there I go again. How am I supposed to do this? Do I just pretend that I didn't spend all that time with him? Do I pretend that I wasn't in love with him? Ugh.

Anyway, back to my new client. All my communication has been done through his assistant Melanie. According to her, they heard Summer Interiors is the best in Connecticut. (I may or may not have danced around my office when she said this because business has been slow this year.) So from what I can tell, Alexander's story is that he just moved into a new home and he's in need of a decorator. However, I get the feeling there's more to the story than just that because, as I said, I did a little background checking. Disclaimer: I need to know what I'm walking into—you just never know what kind of crazy you might find, especially going into someone's home. I send one last reminder invite to both Melanie and Alexander, and I close my laptop. This job really couldn't have come at a better time with my relationship ending the way it did, and since Jake's so ready to move on, so am I.

"Damn, you weren't kidding; he totally looks like Clark Kent," Angie says as she holds my phone close to her face and squints. "Jake who?" she says with a wink.

Yeah, right. There's no way that's happening. If only it was so easy to just forget him and move on to someone else. And even if I were to do that, it wouldn't be with a client.

"You need to get your eyes checked, Ang," I scold while ignoring her comment about Jake. This is not the first time we've had this conversation about her squinting. I'm scared to get in a car with her.

"Summer, I told you I have perfect vision. Everyone in my family has perfect vision."

I roll my eyes as she continues talking. "And I told you there is no way in hell that I'm putting any foreign objects in my eyes. Contacts look like torture devices to me."

I giggle. For as open and loud as she is, she's also the biggest baby. I finally had to forbid her from checking WebMD anytime she had to sneeze.

"So, when is your meeting with Clark?" she asks as she takes a bite of her English muffin.

"His name is Alexander, and our meeting is at ten thirty," I say absently as I check my emails. Whew. Just making sure I didn't get a cancellation.

"Whatever," she says, waving her hand. "We need to discuss more important things—like our Halloween costumes."

I smile. I know this may seem silly to some people but Angie and I have dressed up every Halloween since we were in 11th grade. We almost missed one year because we had a huge fight, but she called me crying the night before, begging me to at least dress up for a party we were attending. She must have had a few drinks because she was rambling something about us missing our holiday together would curse all future Halloweens. I thought she was losing it but I'm not one to risk being cursed.

"I already told Brett that I had plans with you on Halloween," she says pointedly. "And he mentioned something about going to play poker. Who plays poker on Halloween, the best night of the year?" she shouts. I pretend to cover my ears just to make a point. Even though I don't need to being that everyone around us turns to stare.

Brett is Angie's boyfriend. At first, I thought he was weird and kind of scary. First of all, he's huge (Incredible Hulk huge) and he shaves his head. My first impression was that he was an MMA fighter but found out he teaches eighth grade history. I would have freaked out if I walked into a class in eighth grade and he was my teacher.

"It's totally cool if you want to hang with Brett that night," I say, even though the thought of being alone on my favorite night of the year is already starting to break my heart.

"Oh stop, seriously," she says, rolling her eyes. "I just told you he's making plans to play poker. Halloween is totally our night, and if you aren't bringing a man, then neither am I."

I give her a grateful smile. I was hoping she'd say that. I realize this will be the first holiday season in a few years that I've been single. Ugh. And let's face it, this is pretty much the worst time to be single, and not because of the whole gift thing. There's nothing better than curling up by a roaring fire with the person you love. And I don't even want to think about New Year's Eve. When I was eighteen, I spent New Year's Eve at a restaurant with my friend and her boyfriend. I acted like a total bitch the entire night because I was feeling sorry for myself. I definitely don't want a repeat of that, so I will do what it takes to avoid that at all costs.

I double-check the time and realize I better get going to my meeting.

"I'm out of here," I say, checking to make sure I have everything. "We will continue our conversation about Halloween later. We still have plenty of time."

"Not that much time," she insists. "The festivities will be here before we know it." She jumps up and gives me a hug. "Anyway, good luck in your meeting. I expect a full report on Clark."

"Alexander," I remind her. Of course, she's not listening to me. No surprise there.

I type the address that Melanie gave me into my GPS. Luckily, New Canaan isn't that far away. When I check my phone one last time before I get on the road, there's a text message from Alexander Williams. (What?)

Looking forward to meeting with you this morning.

I'm totally in shock because I haven't spoken to him once since Melanie contacted me. He hasn't responded to any of the emails I sent, so why now? I admit I was curious before, but now I'm completely intrigued by this man. His text has made me even more excited for what's next. Summer may be over but I'm ready for a fabulous fall and whatever comes my way.

Chapter Two

*W*hen I pull into the circular driveway, I'm in awe. I cruise really slow as I stare out the window at the pristine manicured lawn. The house is stunning but not a gaudy or oversized stunning. I can feel my excitement growing, and I can't wait to get inside and unleash my decorating magic.

Decorating magic . . . yuck. That's a phrase Jake came up with after I decorated his boss's Cape Cod cottage. According to him, my decorating skills were the talk of his office for months. I even got a few other jobs out of it, and he received all kinds of recognition because of me. I grip the steering wheel a little tighter as my frustration grows thinking about Jake.

I pull up close to the front door behind a sleek silver Audi. Taking a few cleansing breaths, I walk toward the door and ring the bell. I laugh because the doorbell tone sounds a lot like Guns N' Roses "Welcome to the Jungle." Should I be concerned?

A short, blonde girl with a round face meets me at the door. "Hi, Summer, I'm Melanie," she says as she holds out her hand. Wow, she's really short. I feel like a giant at my average 5'6" height. I guess I could have worn something other than these wedges.

"Great to finally meet you in person," I say cheerfully. It could be my imagination but it sounds like she groans.

"Follow me to Mr. Williams's office." She turns down the hallway to the right. Normally, I would be trying to figure out her strange behavior, but I'm too busy. Too busy looking at the bare walls, the circular wrought iron staircase, and the wooden beams in the kitchen. Wow. The possibilities will be endless with this place. Houses like this are exactly why I decided to be an interior decorator.

We walk into the office at the end of the long hallway and the first thing I notice is a wall of glass windows overlooking the beautiful garden. It reminds me a little of an English estate, except on a much smaller scale. The other walls in the office are bare except for a built-in bookshelf to the right when you walk in. Alexander is nowhere to be seen, and I'm starting to wonder if this guy even exists.

"Mr. Williams will be here shortly," she says in a cold, curt tone. "Can I get you a cup of tea or coffee?"

I smile and shake my head. "No, I'm fine, but thank you." There's no way in hell I'm taking a drink from this girl. Judging by the cold reception I've received, I would be afraid she would spit in it or maybe even poison it. Okay, so I know that's silly, but I can read people really well and this girl doesn't like me. Maybe she lured me into this house on purpose; I still haven't seen Mr. Williams. I'm really confused because she seemed fine the few times I spoke to her and her emails were always pleasant. I guess it's possible that she's just having a bad day.

I sit down on the edge of one of the big leather chairs to wait for Mr. Williams. The furniture is rustic and comfortable (and expensive). I look out the window over the sprawling yard. Wow, I would love to have a view like this.

"I apologize for keeping you waiting," a voice says from behind me. I stand up and turn around. Holy crap— Alexander Williams does exist and he looks just like his profile picture.

"Oh, um, no problem. I . . . just arrived," I stutter. I don't know why I'm feeling so nervous all of a sudden. He sits down at his desk, and I study his face for a few seconds. Immediately I notice his friendly smile and dark wavy hair, and he really does resemble Clark Kent. I take a breath and count to five.

"Your home is stunning," I say with a confident tone in my

voice. "Of course, it's missing a few touches that will really bring out its charm. But, that's what I'm here for."

He nods as he takes a sip of his coffee (I'm sure Melanie didn't poison his drink). "It is a great house. I've only been here about three months. After my divorce, I started looking outside the city for something a little quieter. My mother grew up in Ridgefield, and I've always loved Connecticut. As soon as I saw it, I had a feeling this was the right place for me."

So, he's recently divorced? Very interesting. This is not the first new bachelor I've worked with. I wonder why he chose such a big house for just himself.

"So, you're from the city?" I ask.

He nods. "Originally from Westchester but moved to the city after college. My ex-wife and I lived in Tribeca."

I observe him as he mentions the ex-wife. No cringing, no profanity, and no name-calling—maybe they ended amicably. Good for them.

"I love Manhattan," I exclaim. "I actually thought about relocating there, but I just never made the move. I'm close enough to visit, so I guess that's the best of both worlds."

"I agree," he says, flashing me another warm smile. "I love it, too, but I just needed a change."

"Alexander," Melanie interrupts. "Your eight o'clock had to move to ten tomorrow." So she calls him Alexander, but when she spoke to me, she referred to him as Mr. Williams. I think I'm seeing the problem here. Melanie has a big time crush on her boss and she sees me as another woman who's getting ready to spend a lot of time in his home.

"Thanks, Melanie," he replies. "Can you get Ms. Peters something to drink?"

"No, I'm fine," I interrupt. "She already offered me something." I give Melanie a friendly wave, but she pretends not to notice. One thing is for sure—if Melanie is his right hand person, I need to get on her good side. I don't need any drama to get in the way of this job.

This time Melanie doesn't leave the office. She plants herself with her iPad to my right, barely looking at me. I remind myself not to take it personally. I'm here to do my job and that's it.

"Well, shall we get started?" I ask. All my stuttering and nervousness has disappeared and I'm ready to work my magic. Crap! I really need to come up with something else. Unfortunately, the cute phrase has been tainted by a bad breakup.

"Which rooms are you interested in decorating?" I ask, as I get ready to make some notes. I look around his office. "We could start in here," I say, standing up. "Honestly, I wouldn't change the paint color and this furniture is gorgeous. It really just needs some extra touches." I turn toward him and he's staring at me.

Melanie notices it, too, and rolls her eyes. I'm definitely going to have to do some kissing up to get on her good side.

"That sounds great," he replies. "And as far as the rooms I want you to decorate, I say all of them."

Um . . . what?

"All . . . as in the whole house?" I ask, dumbfounded. I glance at Melanie, who looks as shocked as I feel. At least she's not shooting daggers at me with her eyes anymore.

"Are you up for the job or is that too much?" he asks, sounding a little worried.

That's a ridiculous question. Of course I'm up for it.

"Yes. Of course," I respond eagerly. "Melanie said you've checked my references and have seen some of my work.

He smiles. "I have. And you come very highly recommended."

I consider getting up and doing a little dance but that wouldn't be very professional. Instead, I reach out to shake his hand.

"Well, then, I guess we have a deal, Mr. Williams," I say as calmly as I can.

"We only have a deal if you call me Alexander."

I smile. "Okay, only if you call me Summer."

We laugh and Melanie forces a smile. Oh, wow, this is going to be fun.

I'm in a great mood for the first time in weeks. My meeting at Alexander's went very well, and this is the perfect project to distract me from my recent relationship drama. We've decided to start with his office like I suggested, and I presented him with a list of possible ideas. He was very friendly and flirtatious, and I admit I had to stop myself from flirting back. Melanie sat there sulking most of the time but did offer up a few suggestions. I went out of my way to welcome those suggestions because chances are I will be spending more time with Melanie than Alexander. I try to count up the hours that I will be spending at his place. Considering he wants me to decorate the whole house, it looks like I will be around for a while.

Even though I work on location most of the time, I share an office space with my friend Gina. Gina is a telemarketer for three different companies and spends more time in the office than I do.

"Oh my gawsh. You look sooo tan," she says with her thick New Jersey accent. "Tell me all about your vacation."

I set my stuff down and pull my laptop out of my bag. Gina must read my blank expression.

"Oh no, what happened?"

"What makes you think something happened?" I reply sarcastically.

She folds her arms and sits back in her chair. "Oh puh-lease. I can tell when a man does something stupid to affect my friends. So spill."

And that's exactly what I do. I tell her all about Jake and his quick and easy breakup. She shakes her head angrily the whole time.

"Let me tell you something," she snaps. "That bastard is going to get his, you just wait. You know I'm more than happy to make a phone call if you want."

I throw my head back in laughter. Gina loves to offer her, um . . . family's assistance in situations like this. When I first met her, I thought she was exaggerating her family connections; little did I know, she was dead serious. Last year, I had a client who wouldn't pay me. I tried everything I could think of to collect, but they continued to ignore me. I would complain to Gina constantly about it, and finally, I was at my wit's end. She made one call to her Uncle Dominick and the next day I received the payment from my client.

"Thanks, Gina, but I think I just need to get over it and move on. Besides, no one can force Jake to want to be with me."

She unwraps a piece of gum and shoves it in her mouth. "Wanna bet?"

I let out a giggle.

"I'm kidding," she says. "But in case you change your mind, you know I got your back."

I give her a grateful smile. "I appreciate that."

I open my laptop and start to organize my notes for Alexander's house while I listen to Gina making her calls. She sounds like such a different person on the phone, her Jersey accent is barely noticeable.

"What are you working on so intently?" she asks a few minutes later. She's looking over my shoulder at my notes. I feel my excitement start to rise when I think about this new project.

I tell her all about Alexander's offer and about Melanie.

"I need to see this man," she insists. "Pull up his Facebook picture."

I type his name in the search box and turn the screen toward her. She raises her eyebrows.

"Oh, hell yeah," she yells. "I think he's just what you need to forget about Jake and that stupid decorating magic crap."

I start to laugh hysterically because I totally forgot about that. One afternoon Jake had come by the office and he was incessantly bragging to Gina about my decorating magic. He was really proud of that saying, and for some reason, she thought it was really stupid.

"I was just thinking about the magic thing this morning," I tell her. She doesn't say anything being that she's too busy nosing through Alexander's pictures.

"So, what do you think about this hottie?" she asks, pointing to the computer screen.

I shrug casually. "He's seems really nice," I say with a sheepish grin. "But he's recently divorced, so I'm not sure it would be a good idea considering it would be a rebound thing for both of us. That is assuming he would ever be interested in me."

She throws her arms up in frustration. "That's even more reason to give it a shot," she yells. "You both need a good distraction."

"Um . . . that's probably a bad idea," I say. "Especially because he's my client and this is huge for my career. That has to be my number one priority. Not to mention his assistant doesn't like me at all."

Gina gives me a curious look. "Why doesn't she like you?"

I shrug my shoulders. "I honestly have no idea. She seemed fine when I first spoke to her but not today. If looks could kill, I would be dead. I have a theory, though."

She raises her eyebrows. "What's your theory?"

I lean back in my chair. "I think she may have a little crush on her boss . . . or maybe she was just having a bad day?"

"Well, that would totally make sense; she's probably threatened by you. Just remember my offer still stands about the phone call. We can take care of both Jake and this Melanie chick." I laugh as I get up to give her a hug.

"Thanks. I promise I will let you know."

I get back to my work, and after Gina leaves for the day, I receive an email from Alexander.

Dear Summer,

It was great meeting you today. I'm looking forward to working with you and finally making my house a home. I will not be able to make it to the meeting on Friday after all, but Melanie will be there to assist you with anything you need. I look forward to seeing your ideas come to life.

Alexander

I make a face. I guess Melanie and I are going to have to figure out a way to coexist because it's clear she's not going anywhere and neither am I.

I guess I've been putting this off. Subconsciously, picking up Jake's key is the last reminder that things are over between us. I stopped by Mrs. Rothera's place when I got back from the beach trip, but she wasn't home. I still can't believe he left it with her just to avoid having to see me.

Mrs. Rothera owns the building, and she fits the typical nosy neighbor profile perfectly. To be honest, she kind of makes me nervous, so I don't have much to do with her other than paying my rent and typical maintenance requests.

I knock loudly on her door. No answer. Just as I turn to leave, she opens the door.

"Hello, Summer," she says. My eyes immediately focus on her outfit. It looks like she's wearing some kind of costume. It's a colorful dress with beaded fringe and a matching headscarf. She looks like a gypsy. Maybe she's preparing for Halloween, too. Angie would love it.

"I'm sorry if I'm catching you at a bad time," I say as I drag my eyes away from her headscarf.

"Not a bad time at all," she replies. "Just preparing for an event I'm attending this evening. Come on in."

She opens the door wide and ushers me in. She's attending an event dressed like that? I guess her idea of appropriate attire would differ from mine—depending on the type of event.

"I suppose you're here for this," she says, holding up my key. It's still on the key chain from our cruise to St. Thomas. Ugh. He didn't even keep the key chain.

I give her a weak smile. "Yes. Thank you." She cocks her head to the side and gives me a funny look.

"Why don't you come and sit down for a minute? Can I get you something to drink?"

"No thank you," I reply. "I just got off work, and I haven't even been home yet."

She looks at me with pity. "Dinner for one."

Ouch. That was a harsh reminder. As if it's her business anyway. There she goes again, sticking her nose in where it doesn't belong. I suck in a deep breath because I know I need to be nice to her considering she is my landlord.

"Yes," I say shortly.

"He will be back," she says under her breath. What did she say? Did she say he would be back? He . . . as in Jake?

"I'm sorry. What was that?" I ask.

"Your boyfriend. He will be back. I've seen it." She sits down at the table and that's when I notice the stuff covering her table. Cards, books, charts, and crystals . . . who is this woman?

She notices me staring at her table. "Have you ever had a reading?"

My eyes grow big. "A reading? Like from a fortune teller?"

She laughs loudly. "Not a fortune teller. A psychic reading."

I shake my head. The truth is, I've always been curious about psychics, but I'm too much of a chicken to ever go to one. I'm not sure I'm willing to open that door . . . or portal or whatever it's called.

"How about it?" she asks, pointing to the chair next to her. Hmmm . . . I may be curious about it but not curious enough to go to some amateur. I've lived in this building for over a year. How is it that I'm just finding this out about her now?

"You're a psychic?" I ask, trying to hide my skepticism.

She nods proudly. "Yes."

Okay, I guess she woke up one morning and said, "Hey, I think I will be a psychic today." This is really awkward, mainly because I don't believe her. Although, I keep my mouth shut because I definitely don't want to hurt her feelings. She certainly looks the part with her fancy new outfit, and I can see she has all the tools a psychic would have, but that doesn't mean she is one.

"You don't believe me," she says. Okay, so she figured that out, still doesn't prove anything. "That's okay. All in good time," she adds.

What does she mean by that? I feel like everything out of her mouth is some kind of hidden message.

"It's not that I don't believe you," I reply. "I just didn't know. I mean, you never said anything."

She fixes her headscarf and rearranges the things on her table. "It's not something I just announce to people. It has to be the appropriate time." She pauses. "Anyway, when you're ready, I will be here. But let me just give you one piece of advice." She closes her eyes.

I look around, waiting for something strange to happen. Maybe the chair will shake or she will start chanting . . . but nothing happens.

She opens her eyes and looks directly at me. "When he comes around, trust your instincts."

I wait for her to finish. But she doesn't say anything else.

"And . . ." I ask.

She shrugs. "That's all for now."

What does she mean *that's all for now?*

"Oh except, don't forget the pest control is on Friday," she says as she stands up.

Is this a joke? She goes from giving me some important information about my life to talking about the pest control? I don't move from where I'm standing, but she's obviously done as she gathers her things and starts filling a tote bag.

I thank her for the key, but I'm still confused as I walk up the stairs to my apartment. What just happened? Did she give me an important clue to my future? Is Jake going to try to reconcile? I'm wondering if I just had my first psychic reading.

Chapter Three

I pull the phone away from my ear because Angie is yelling. "Holy crap, can you turn your volume down?" I snap. "I'm going deaf over here."

"So what do you think? Those are fun costumes, right?" she says, toning down her voice but not addressing my demand.

"Honestly, it's been done," I reply. She suggested doing the whole *Grease* Pink Ladies theme again and I'm just not feeling it.

"Come on, we did that over ten years ago, people have forgotten by now." I know Angie is getting frustrated with me. I've shot down all of her costume ideas so far.

"How about a tootsie roll and gum ball machine?" she says sarcastically. "Or maybe *you* should come up with some ideas."

I feel bad. The truth is I've been distracted since my visit with Mrs. Rothera. After I left her place, I started recalling different interactions I've had with her. I always thought she was nosy, like she was watching us come and go or maybe listening through the air vents. The thought never crossed my mind that she had secret powers to see things happening.

"We'll think of something," I tell her. "We still have time," I say, glancing at my calendar.

"You keep saying that, and we don't have that much time, especially if we want to plan a party," she says innocently. Party? Who said anything about a party?

"No way. I don't think so," I tell her. "I'm about to start a huge project with work. The last thing I need to do is commit to planning a party."

I hear pots and pans banging around in the background. "Don't worry. I will do the planning, and it will be awesome. We just have to find a place to have it."

Hah! I know what she means by that; in other words, I have to find a place to have it.

"I don't know . . ." I trail off.

"Come on, it will be fun, and what better way to celebrate your exciting new single life than a Halloween party. It would be the perfect place to meet someone."

Okay, on that note, it's time for me to end this call. I check the time. I have to meet Melanie in forty-five minutes. We've been communicating back and forth via email for the last few days, and it's like she's a different person than the one I met at Alexander's. I'm hoping that she's accepted the fact that I'm going to be around for a while, meaning while I'm decorating (not because of Alexander). Otherwise, this is going to be a long few months.

"Oh fine, plan the party but remember this is all you." I agree. "Oh, and no tootsie roll or gum ball machine costumes."

She snickers. "Deal."

How does Angie always talk me into this stuff? The last brilliant idea she had was starting an online travel planning company. I thought she was crazy, but I'm happy to say that Friendship Travel is still doing very well. Angie is now running it by herself. I became hands-off when business started picking up for Summer Interiors. Angie has always embraced her entrepreneurial spirit, even in high school when she made a killing with friendship bracelets and headbands. Maybe a Halloween party won't be so bad, if anything, it's something else to look forward to.

I don't know what kind of game this girl is playing. I've been waiting outside Alexander's house for fifteen minutes and Melanie is nowhere to be found. After pounding on the door for the third time, she finally opens it.

"There you are," she says. "I just sent Alexander a message asking if he heard from you. I thought you were a no-show."

Is she kidding?

"Melanie, I've been here for fifteen minutes," I say emphatically. "I called and texted you, and I've been pounding on the door."

She gives me a doubtful look. "I didn't get anything." She pauses. "Oh well, you're here now."

She holds the door open for me. I could stand here and argue with her, but I know it's not worth it. I walk into the house and she closes the door behind me.

I follow her into the kitchen. She sits down at the table where her laptop is open. I set up right next to her, and she's watching me the whole time. It's a little awkward for a few moments, but rather than draw any attention to it, I get right to work. I need to try my best to let her know that I'm here to do my job, and I have no intention of stealing her crush away.

"Since we're starting with the office, this is what I came up with. This is exactly what I was talking to Alexander about," I say, turning my laptop toward her. She looks and nods her head. She's obviously impressed but I'm not expecting her to admit it.

"What do you think?" I ask, trying to make it sound like her opinion is very important. I hate kissing up to her, but I don't know what else to do.

"Nice," she replies. I think I notice a tiny trace of a smile. She quickly goes back to her computer.

"So, how long have you worked with Alexander?" I ask, trying to make conversation.

I should have known that a mention of their relationship (professional or not) would make her more willing to talk.

"We've worked together for three years," she says with a smile (a real smile this time). "I did my internship with his company and I was assigned to work with Alexander. Upon completion of the internship, I was offered a position with his company but I stayed with him. I can't beat the pay or the freedom."

I nod. "Freedom is a big deal. Being able to make your own schedule is awesome."

She's looking at something on her laptop and her expression changes. And just like that the wall comes down again. I don't know what changed all of a sudden.

"Is everything okay?" I ask her.

She gets up from the table. "Yep. Just great."

We work silently for the next hour. I walk around the house, taking some pictures and measurements. I'm busy making notes in one of the guest rooms when I hear a man's voice.

"Hi, Summer," Alexander says as he walks into the room, and for a few seconds, I feel my pulse speed up. This is a welcome surprise. Not only because he looks amazing in his suit, but I don't know how much more of Melanie's silence and cold shoulder I can take today.

"What are you doing here?"

He clasps his hands. "My appointments didn't last as long as I expected, so I was able to make it home earlier. I sent Melanie a message, didn't she tell you?"

So that explains her sudden change of attitude. I've gone out of my way to be nice to her, so I'm not sure what else I can do. When Alexander and I head back to the kitchen, Melanie is slumped over the table.

"Summer has a great eye. So far she's living up to her name," he announces. I sit back down at the table and Melanie doesn't acknowledge me. Alexander excuses himself to change his clothes, and rather than waste my time forcing a conversation, I don't say anything to Melanie.

When Alexander returns to the kitchen, my mouth drops open so I quickly cover my mouth with my hand. He's changed into a pair of sweatpants and a T-shirt that clings to his chest. I notice that Melanie is watching my reaction out of the corner of my eye, so I drag my attention away from Alexander and his toned physique.

Before I know it, five o'clock rolls around and I'm still working. We've gone through every room from ceiling to floor. Melanie left around four and it was very obvious she was hoping I would be leaving at the same time.

"You must be starving," Alexander says. "Would you like me to order something . . . or do you have to leave?"

Hmm . . . believe it or not, this is a difficult decision. I could stay here and have dinner in this beautiful kitchen or I could go home to my lonely, empty apartment. Not to mention possibly running into Mrs. Rothera and her new magical psychic powers. At the same time, staying here would go against my plan of staying focused on this job and not crossing over into a nonprofessional situation. Before I can respond, he's on the phone ordering food from a local Greek restaurant. I guess I'm staying for dinner.

I shouldn't be having this much fun, but I am. First of all, Alexander ordered the most amazing Greek food. I feel like an absolute pig because I have devoured everything. I'm really enjoying hanging out with Alexander; he's nice and really down-to-earth. Come to think of it, he's nothing like I expected he would be when they first contacted me about this job. I guess I was expecting someone more hands-off and distant.

"Are you happy living in the suburbs? It's a big difference from city life," I say, taking another bite of my baklava. I have a feeling I will be frequenting It's All Greek quite often after this evening.

He nods. "I'm enjoying the quiet, that's for sure. But it does get a little lonely being that all my friends are still in the city."

We're interrupted by the sound of my phone buzzing. I've been ignoring my phone for most of the evening.

"Sorry. I should check my messages." When I look at it, I have three texts and one voice mail from Angie. I have no doubt she's in full Halloween-planning mode.

"Everything okay?" he asks. "I'm sorry if I've kept you for too long."

I shake my head. "Oh, it's totally fine. It's just my friend Angie; she's obsessing over Halloween. It's nothing unusual."

His eyes light up. "I don't blame her. Halloween is my favorite holiday." I stare at him intently. This guy is officially too good to be true—first *Grease 2* and now Halloween.

"I totally agree, but Angie just has more free time on her hands than I do and she seems to forget that a lot." I tell him all about our years of celebrating Halloween and about her idea to actually throw a party this year.

"She promised she'd plan the whole night and all I'd have to do is find a place to host it." I take a sip of my water.

Alexander gives a thoughtful look. "You can have it here if you want," he says nonchalantly. I'm so shocked by his offer that I spit my water out all over the table.

"Oh crap. I'm sorry," I say as I quickly wipe the table. "Alexander, I appreciate your offer but that's a huge undertaking."

He holds up his hands. "No, it's really not. My ex and I hosted parties all the time in the city. And didn't I just tell you I was lonely? I would love to meet some new people, and I could invite some friends to come down from the city."

He's totally serious. I don't know what to say.

"There is one thing . . ." He hesitates. "Do you think we could have a few of the rooms decorated by then? At least downstairs."

I open my calendar. "I think so. I will have to get items ordered ASAP, but I think it's do-able."

He smiles excitedly. "That's great. I think a party is exactly what I need."

"Me, too. We could do some amazing fall and Halloween décor. I mean, if you want. Although Angie should be taking care of decorations," I add.

He nods as he picks up his phone. "Sounds good. Now I just have to come up with a good costume."

For some reason, Jake pops into my head right at that moment. Why does this happen at the worst time? My mind wanders back to last Halloween. Jake was such a pain about dressing up for an event we were all attending. Of course, Angie and I had our plan and Jake just wanted to wear a shirt that said, "This Is My Costume."

"Maybe I can get a few friends to dress up as the T-Birds from *Grease*," he says, snapping me out of my Jake daydream.

I try to hide my enthusiasm when he mentions *Grease*.

"You like *Grease*?" I ask, trying to act surprised. It's not like I'm going to admit that I already knew that because I stalked him online.

He hangs his head. "Yeah . . . are you going to take my man card?"

I start to laugh. "I'm not sure."

"And to be fair, I like *Grease 2* more. It's my favorite movie of all time," he says.

I pretend to be shocked.

"Let me guess . . . Michelle Pfeiffer?" I say as I roll my eyes.

He snorts. "Of course."

I knew it.

"You want to hear something funny," I say, folding my napkin in my hand for the hundredth time. "Angie just mentioned us wearing Pink Ladies costumes. We did it like ten years ago and I told her it was played out."

He leans back in shock. "I can't believe you just said that. The movie is a classic. It will never be played out. Maybe you should consider it. We would probably look great together." He stops talking suddenly, and I shift around in my seat. I know he didn't mean to say that the way it came out.

My phone rings again just in time to startle me. Sure enough, it's Angie again.

"I probably should answer."

He nods quickly. "Absolutely. And give her the good news." He gets up from the table and starts to clean up the dishes.

I try to contain my excitement as I watch Alexander walk around his kitchen. I have a feeling this Halloween is going to be one of the best yet.

Chapter Four

The next morning, I wake up extra early and lie in my bed for a few minutes. I think back over the events of yesterday. Professionally speaking, it was a great day with the exception of Melanie and her dirty looks. I got a lot accomplished at the house, and I have a good plan in place to get the rooms downstairs decorated before the party. On a personal level, I made a new friend, and that's always a bonus. The nice thing is that I didn't feel any pressure. Spending time with Alexander was like hanging with a good friend.

Angie was ecstatic when I told her about Alexander offering his house for the Halloween Bash, and of course she wanted to speak to him. I started laughing hysterically when he pulled the phone a few inches from his ear and I could still hear every word. I also cringed when she invited him to join us for lunch next week. She says it was to discuss the party, but I've been friends with her long enough to know that the curiosity is killing her and she wants to meet him in person. Not that I blame her, because regardless of him looking like Clark Kent (which he does), he's really funny. He agreed to join us for lunch after he checked his schedule (the schedule Melanie keeps for him).

Speaking of Melanie, he did make a strange comment about her. I can't remember how she came up, but I mentioned how dedicated she is to her job and his response was "almost too dedicated." I didn't want to pry, but it doesn't take a genius to know what he meant by that remark. Regardless, she still works with him after three years so he obviously doesn't mind her dedication. He would be a complete moron not to see how she feels about him, or he could just be a typical man.

Thankfully, after my eventful day yesterday, I will be running errands today so I won't be seeing Melanie or Alexander. I think I will let him break the news to her about his offer to host our Halloween party. It will probably be better if I'm far away from that conversation.

I'm about to walk out the door when Angie shows up at my door. She's wearing a tank top that says, "Yoga and Gangster Rap." Somehow she always finds these cute and quirky things.

"Nice shirt. What are you doing here?" I ask, folding my arms. I really have to get to work, so I don't have time to chat (or listen).

She walks past me and into my apartment. "Can't I pay my best friend a visit?"

I look at my watch. "At nine o'clock in the morning? You know you could have called me."

She completely ignores me and walks into the kitchen and opens my refrigerator. I don't mind because we do this all the time. I'm just waiting patiently for her to ask me about last night.

"So," she says.

I start to laugh. "So. Really, that's all you have to say? Seriously, just ask me."

The corner of her mouth curls up. "Okay, tell me HOW you persuaded your new client to host our Halloween party. I'm impressed, by the way."

She pours herself a glass of orange juice and takes a sip. I lean against the counter. "I didn't persuade him. He was telling me about moving out of the city and how it's been lonely. You started texting me about the party and I told him. He offered to have the party there. That's it."

She looks at me in awe. "You're good."

"Ang, I'm telling you the truth. I didn't do anything. Can we discuss this later? I really need to get to work."

She puts her glass in the sink. "Fine. But when are we going to talk about the plans?"

I hold up my hand. "Uh-uh . . . I did my part. I found a location. You said you would do everything else."

There is no way I'm letting her rope me into doing any party planning. Especially because now I have to get Alexander's house ready.

"I know, and I will take care of the party details. But, we still need to talk about our costumes."

The mention of costumes reminds me of Alexander and the Pink Ladies/T-Bird theme. I'm trying not to overreact to what he said, but I did enjoy hanging out with him and I have no doubt that he's usually the life of the party.

On our way out, we meet Mrs. Rothera in the hallway. I haven't seen her since her whole "I'm a psychic" reveal.

"Hello, ladies."

"Hi, Mrs. Rothera," we say politely.

"Summer, have you thought any more about coming to see me for the reading?" she asks. Wow, she's not wasting any time. I wish she wouldn't have said anything in front of Angie.

"You're welcome to come as well," she says, pointing at Angie.

"What are you reading?" Angie asks.

Ugh. I don't want to talk about this.

"I do psychic readings," Mrs. Rothera says proudly.

Angie looks back and forth between Mrs. Rothera and me. She's probably wondering why I didn't tell her sooner. This is exactly the kind of information that Angie loves.

"You do," she says excitedly. "Oh my gosh, you have to come to our Halloween party."

My mouth drops open. She can't be serious. Actually, I know Angie and she's totally serious. They start talking and I feel like I'm dreaming.

"I really have to go," I interrupt. "I will let you two work this out." They stop talking long enough to say good-bye and Mrs. Rothera reminds me to stop by to visit her.

When I get in my car, I think about everything that's happened over the last few days (and weeks). Maybe Mrs. Rothera can give me some insight into Alexander. And what about Jake? The last time I spoke to her she mentioned him coming back. I don't know what I would do if Jake came back or if I could get past the pain he caused me. Hmmm . . . maybe I don't want to know if he's coming back.

~

I haven't spoken to Alexander (other than a few texts) since I left his place last week. Not that it's any of my business, but I know he's been working some really long hours. At least, that's what Melanie has told me. I have no doubt that she knows about the Halloween party because the tone of her emails has gotten worse. Emotion is usually harder to read in emails and texts but definitely not in hers. On a good note, I'm making great progress with the house. I was able to order quite a bit of the furniture, lighting, and wall décor. And, of course, Melanie has been right behind me to double-check and make sure every detail is perfect. I'm sure the girl is praying that I will mess something up.

Today is the day that Alexander is joining Angie and me for lunch. Normally I would be worried but for some reason I'm not. I've already made Angie promise that she wouldn't tell any embarrassing stories about me, and I've got so much dirt on her that I know she will keep her word.

As far as the Halloween party, her planning is in full swing, and much to my dismay, she has invited Mrs. Rothera to come, not as a guest but as a psychic. I know it's not a big deal but something about this whole thing makes me nervous. Maybe it's the possibility of hearing something I'm not going to like.

When I arrive at the café, Angie is already there and she's talking loudly on her phone. She waves at me as soon as I sit down.

"YES," she shouts. "That's right, about a hundred people. Perfect."

One hundred people for what? There's no way she could be talking about the party . . . right?

I don't give her a chance to say hi before asking her about the guest list.

"You weren't talking about the party, were you?" I demand.

She gives me a blank look. "Um, yeah. Why?"

Holy crap.

"One hundred people," I shout. "We can't invite that many to Alexander's house."

She looks at me as if I've lost my mind.

"Of course we can."

I place my face in my hands. Maybe he won't care, but I'm embarrassed. She hasn't even met him yet and she's ready to invite the whole tri-state area to his house.

"Summer, relax. I'll ask him when he gets here," she says calmly. "I promised you I would handle everything and I will. You just sit there and look pretty."

I giggle despite being completely annoyed with her. "Very funny. Remember, we are just friends. And speaking of friends, have you spoken to Mrs. Rothera?"

Before she has a chance to respond, Alexander shows up.

"Is this seat taken?" he asks playfully.

Angie raises her eyebrows, and I can read her expression. I can tell that she's already impressed with him. And I don't blame her a bit. He looks very dashing today with his glasses and tailored shirt. His tie is loosened, and for some reason, I think that is so sexy.

"Hi, Alexander," I say cheerfully. "This is my friend Angie."

"Oh, stop the formality," Angie exclaims. "We're old friends." She stands up and holds her arms out to give him a hug. And of course, being the nice guy he is, he hugs her back.

Formality or not, he's still my client but I know she doesn't care about that.

"Great to finally meet you in person, Angie," he says with a big grin on his face. He turns toward me and rubs my shoulder. "And it's good to see you, Summer."

I try not to overreact to his hand on my shoulder. Especially since Angie is already doing that as she's watching our interaction very closely. I give her a look that clearly says, "Keep your mouth shut and we will talk about it later."

"Okay, so let's get down to business," Angie says, following my lead. "Here are our plans so far."

For the next hour, we talk about the party, or rather, Angie and Alexander talk about it. I mostly listen and give a few suggestions. I have to admit it sounds like it's going to be a blast.

"Wait a second," Alexander interrupts, looking at Angie's notes. "You hired a fortune teller?" He starts laughing after Angie tells him about Mrs. Rothera.

"She's actually a psychic," I tell him. "At least she is now." I explain to them about how I just thought she was really nosy and that I just found out about her little secret.

"Well, I'm interested to hear what she has to say about my future," he says, giving me an innocent look.

Luckily, Angie chimes in at just the right time to break up what could have been a very awkward moment. She wants Mrs. Rothera to have a good spot so the guests can visit her if they want to. I begin to daydream as we continue to discuss the party. I can't believe I'm letting this happen. I never thought I would be interested in a client. I know it could be a total rebound thing or that he's just a really great guy. Either way, this is very unprofessional. Not only that, there's still so much I don't know about him, like how long was he married? Why did he get divorced? These are important questions. Of course, I'm totally jumping to conclusions here—just because I have a crush on him doesn't mean he has one on me.

"Jake?"

My daydream is interrupted when I hear Angie say Jake's name. My heart sinks. What the . . . ?

I turn around to see Jake standing behind me. He looks

right at me and immediately a rush of different emotions comes over me.

"Hi, Angie. Hi, Summer," he says awkwardly.

"Hello, Jake," I reply. It came out colder than I intended, but after the way he hauled butt out of my life, I guess I'm entitled to that reaction. We're all quiet for a few seconds until I remember that Alexander is sitting with us. He's watching our interaction carefully.

"Alexander, this is Jake."

Alexander, being the nice guy he is, gets up to shake his hand.

"Alexander just moved to Connecticut from the city," I say. "He's hired me to decorate his house."

"And she's doing a great job already," he says proudly. I can feel myself start to blush.

Jake gives a sheepish grin. "I have no doubt. I've always said Summer has decorating magic."

I cringe as memories begin flooding back. Angie is watching the whole scene. I know she's holding back from going off on Jake.

"We're in the middle of planning a big Halloween party," Angie interrupts. She obviously noticed my discomfort. "Alexander was nice enough to offer to host the party at his new home."

Alexander shrugs his shoulders. "I'm happy to. It's a great way to meet people in a new town. You should come, Jake."

Angie and I look at each other in horror. I know it's not Alexander's fault, being that he doesn't know our history, but the thought of Jake crashing this party makes me nauseous.

"Um . . . maybe," Jake replies as looks at his watch. "I'm sorry, but I have to get to a meeting. It was nice seeing you two and great meeting you, Alex."

"Alexander," he corrects him.

"Uh . . . yeah, sorry. Good-bye."

Jake practically runs away. I rub my temples vigorously because that pretty much sucked. I knew I was bound to run into Jake at some point but I never imagined it would be that torturous. Alexander is eyeing me curiously.

"Okay, so do one of you want to tell me what that was about?" he asks. "I'm really sorry if I overstepped by inviting him. I figured you all were friends."

Yeah, friends, I think to myself.

"It's okay," I assure him. "We're not exactly friends . . . Jake is my ex-boyfriend."

Poor Alexander cringes.

"Oh man, I'm sorry," he exclaims. "And I just invited him to the party."

"Don't worry about it," Angie interrupts. "He won't show his face at this party, and if he does, he won't be there for long."

I nod in agreement. "No, he won't. But don't feel bad, it's fine . . . and I'm fine."

I really am fine . . . I think. In my defense, it was the first time I've seen him since he left the beach. It was bound to bring up some emotion. If anything, I think it was better having Angie and Alexander with me so I didn't have to face him on my own.

Shortly after we finish lunch, Angie leaves to run some errands. Alexander and I walk out together.

"So, I'm not trying to pry into your life and you don't have to tell me anything. I'm just curious about what happened with you and that Jake guy."

I stare at the sidewalk before making eye contact with him.

"We broke up over the summer," I say as nonchalantly as I can. He chews on his bottom lip as I continue. "Or rather, he broke up with me over the summer . . . at the beach . . . while we were on vacation. No explanation, just that he wasn't ready for anything serious—even though we had been serious for quite some time."

I hate to make it seem like I'm still bothered by this, but I would be lying if I acted like I wasn't.

He lets out a slow whistle. "Oh . . . that's harsh."

"Sorry to unload like that," I tell him. "I usually don't share my personal life with clients, but since you asked."

He nervously shifts from one foot to another. I get the feeling he wants to say something.

"Is everything okay?" I ask him.

He nods slowly. "Yeah. I just wanted to tell you that I think of you as a friend." He pauses. "I mean, other than you just decorating my house, so don't feel bad about giving me the scoop. And I'm the one who asked. I could sense something was off, and then I open my big mouth and invite him to the party." He shakes his head.

I put my hand on his arm. "It's okay. And I appreciate you saying that we're friends. I feel the same way." We're standing, facing each other in the middle of the sidewalk. Just then his phone starts to ring and he quickly grabs it.

"Excuse me for one second," he says as he answers.

"Yes, Melanie," he answers. I turn my face away from him and scowl. That Melanie sure has impeccable timing.

"Okay, I will call him now," he insists.

When he hangs up, he's scrolling through his phone. "I hate to cut this short but I need to take care of something."

"I understand. I actually have to run by your house and check on a delivery," I say. He holds out his hand to shake mine. Well, nothing says just friends like shaking hands.

Chapter Five

I'm exhausted. I've been working long hours at Alexander's for the last few days. I've only seen him for a few minutes as he's been in the city working a lot, which is probably for the best, but I admit I've missed him being around. He's definitely more fun than Melanie.

Unfortunately, Melanie has been around and she has been civil for the most part, with the exception of a snide comment about the Halloween party. She said something about all the "strangers" who were going to be in the house and how Alexander is too nice and that sometimes people take advantage of him. I wanted so badly to put her in her place, but I bit my tongue—again.

When I get home, I'm starving. I'm heating one of those gross Lean Cuisine meals (because I'm too tired to prepare anything else) when there's a knock at my door. I open it to find Mrs. Rothera with a saucepan in her hands.

"Hi," I say, forcing a smile. I really don't want to get into any conversations about my life tonight.

"I hope I'm not bothering you. I made this vegetable soup, and I thought you might be hungry. I have plenty."

Wow. Either she heard me complaining about the frozen meal or she *is* psychic.

"That's very kind of you," I say. I know I can't avoid this woman forever, so I decide to invite her in. "Would you like to come in?" She actually looks surprised but accepts my invite.

When she comes in, she sits down on my couch and I offer her something to drink. Even though I'm not into this psychic thing, I'm curious about what she said about Jake.

After I hand her a glass of water, I ask her the burning question. "I've been wanting to ask you about what you said about Jake. And please don't take this the wrong way, but I'm not really interested in a reading, at least not right now."

She gives me a tight-lipped simile. I hope that didn't come across the wrong way. I'm not trying to piss her off.

"Would any of this have to do with the new man you're spending time with?"

What? How does she know this stuff?

"Well . . . not exactly. You mentioned that Jake would be back, and I wanted to know if you could explain."

She looks around my apartment but doesn't respond for a few seconds. "You don't believe me, do you?"

Now she's staring at me but it feels more like she's staring through me. I don't want to make her feel bad because, honestly, I don't know what I think. She has mentioned things that she wouldn't know unless she has some kind of other sense. Things she couldn't possibly know about.

I hear my phone buzzing from the kitchen. I'm getting a text message, but I decide to ignore it.

"Honestly, I don't know," I reply as I lower my head. "I admit you've known certain things . . ."

She gets up from the chair and sits down on the couch next to me. "To answer your question. Yes, Jake will be back. And in regards to the new man, you should know that there is another woman involved."

What other woman? My phone starts to buzz again.

"You should answer that, and I will let you be," she says as she gets up to leave.

I want to ask her more questions but that's not really fair considering I basically said that I don't believe she has magical powers. "Thank you for the soup," I call as I go to grab my phone.

I almost drop my phone when I see the text. It's from Jake.

I was wondering if we could talk. Let me know.

My legs feel weak, almost like I may pass out. Okay, now I'm freaking out. Did Mrs. Rothera know Jake was texting me? The question is what do I do? Should I listen to what he has to say? The one thing I know is that I can't reply to him tonight. I'm completely exhausted and I need time to think —about everything.

Maybe I do have decorating magic? Alexander's office looks fantastic, if I do say so myself. I stand back and look around proudly. I'm not usually one to toot my own horn but I did a great job with this room. Alexander already had a gorgeous mahogany desk, so I just had to work around that. I found two chaise lounges and they matched perfectly. Then I added some wall décor, an area rug, and some amazing artwork with different views of the New York City skyline. I hope being in here gives him a sense of "home."

I happily wander back into the kitchen and sit down at the table. I've been trying to avoid my phone (mainly the text messages). It's been a few days and I still haven't responded to Jake's text. I know I need to say something, even if I just tell that I'm not ready yet. I hear the front door open; it's probably Melanie because she doesn't like me being at Alexander's house alone for too long. Maybe she thinks I'm going to prance around pretending to be the lady of the house. Not that the thought hasn't crossed my mind, but only because I love it here and not because of Alexander (well, not entirely).

"Hey. I thought you would be gone by already," Alexander says, dropping a bunch of bags on the floor. He looks really tired.

"Oh, I'm almost done," I say worriedly.

"No. I didn't mean it like that," he insists. "You're just working so late, but I'm glad you're still here."

We smile warmly at each other, and I hope that I'm not starting to blush. I'm not going to lie; I really enjoy it when he's home.

"I just finished hanging everything in your office," I say without taking my eyes off him. "Would you like to see it?"

He loosens his tie. *Why is it so hot when men do that?*

"Of course," he exclaims. "Let's see if you live up to your reputation."

I lead the way. I feel like I should do a drum roll or say ta-da, or something.

Alexander walks in and looks around. He turns toward me and nods. "Wow, this is very impressive. I may never want to leave now."

"Thanks," I say proudly.

He leans against the front of his desk and rubs his temples. I don't know why but I get the feeling something is bothering him.

"Alexander, is everything okay?"

He drops his hands. "Yeah, it was just a hectic day at the office. That combined with seeing my ex-wife, I'm worn out."

My curiosity is piqued at the mention of his ex.

"Oh," I reply as I grit my teeth.

He sighs as he sits down on one of the new chaise lounges. "Yeah. Helena can be a handful, to say the least."

My mind starts to wander back to what Mrs. Rothera said about another woman. Maybe she was referring to his ex-wife. I sit down on the edge of one of the chairs.

"If you don't mind me asking, how long were you two married?" I figure now is the best time to ask him. And since he brought her up, it doesn't sound like I'm being nosy. Besides, he asked me about Jake, so I shouldn't feel weird asking about his ex-wife.

He undoes his top two buttons. *First the tie and now the buttons . . . Whew.*

"We were married for four years," he replies. "It was kind of a whirlwind romance. She's originally from Sweden, and she was here working for a modeling agency. We met at a party in the city, and from that night on, we were inseparable."

A Swedish model—I think I've changed my mind about wanting to know more about her.

"The last year and half were rough," he continues. "I guess the intensity between us finally wore off."

I give him a sympathetic look even though I really don't want to hear anymore. I can only imagine what kind of intensity the two of them had.

"When did you divorce?" I ask. I know he's been in the house a few months, but he never mentioned how long he's been divorced.

"Our divorce was final in May, on our fourth anniversary actually."

I scrunch my face. "Oh wow."

"Anyway, we're still friends so it's fine. She stopped by my office today, and as I said, she can be a lot to deal with." I know I shouldn't have this feeling but the thought of Helena the Swedish model spending time with Alexander makes me really jealous.

"And . . . she heard about the Halloween party," he adds. "Unfortunately, we still have a lot of the same friends." Crap. I bite my bottom lip, but there is nothing I can say. This may be our party, but it's Alexander's house.

"I told her about you," he says softly.

I give him a curious look. "You did? What exactly did you tell her?"

He sits up and runs his fingers through his hair. "I told her about you decorating the house." He laughs nervously. "And . . ."

I swallow loudly. "And . . . what?"

He leans his head against the back of the couch. "And I told her that I like spending time with you." My pulse picks up again. He's now looking at me, obviously waiting for me to say something. I have so much going through my mind right now.

"I like spending time with you, too," I reply. The corners of his lips curl into a smile. The next thing I know he's leaning over me and he's kissing me. I start to run my fingers through his hair. I realize how much I've wanted this to happen. At the same time, I feel like we shouldn't be doing this.

All of a sudden, I hear Melanie's voice. "Alexander. Did you get . . . Oh my gosh!" Alexander jumps off the chair and I sit up straight.

She's standing in the doorway with the look of shock on her face. "I'm so sorry," she says quickly and rushes out of the room. I close my eyes and put my face in my hands. This is bad. What was I thinking?

"Hey," he says, tapping me on the shoulder. "Don't worry about her." I nod my head, but I feel horrible. Not only have I broken my own rule of not getting involved with a client, now Melanie will hate me more than she already does.

"You should probably go talk to her," I say as I stand up. "I need to get going anyway."

I start to walk out of the office, but he catches my elbow. "Summer, please don't go yet. I meant what I said."

I smile. "I know, but you need to check on her. We can talk later."

I pack up my laptop and my things, which are strewn all over the table. I'm not sure where Melanie ran off to. As I walk to my car, I almost feel like I'm doing the walk of shame after being caught making out. When I'm safely in my car, I run my fingers across my lips. Wow. I smile to myself. Other than Melanie walking in on us, it couldn't have been any more perfect. One thing is for sure, I also meant what I said. I really enjoy spending time with him, too.

Chapter Six

"Do you like any of these costumes?" Angie asks for the hundredth time. "What do you think, Gina?"

It's Saturday morning and the three of us are having brunch. I'm hardly paying attention being that I'm still in a bit of a daze since my intense encounter with Alexander. He texted me after I left and told me he talked to Melanie and everything was fine. And then he said he was looking forward to continuing our conversation. Conversation? I guess that's one way to describe it.

"I think you should do your own thing," Gina says. "Forget this one over here."

She's pointing at me.

I roll my eyes. Gina dresses the same every Halloween and her costume is always some kind of sexy animal. Meaning lingerie with some kind of animal theme. Last year, she was the sexy tiger.

"I told you they were all fine. You can choose."

She glares at me. "What's your deal? You seem really distracted. Do I need to call Mrs. Rothera here to help?"

I snort. "No way. I have enough going on without being told what my future holds." I pause. "Jake texted me. He wants to talk."

Both of their mouths drop open, and then they both start yelling at exactly the same time. "What? When did this happen?" Angie asks.

"Just let me make one call," Gina exclaims. "One call and this will be taken care of."

I ignore Gina's mention of the phone call. "He texted last week sometime. I haven't responded yet because something else happened since then."

They glance at each other. I guess I made it sound worse than it really is. "Nothing bad," I assure them.

"Well, are you going to tell us?" Angie asks.

I tell them about Alexander and that amazing kiss. And then how the moment was ruined when Melanie interrupted us.

"Not that assistant again," Gina says, sounding exasperated. "Please tell me you aren't letting her get to you."

"Why are you upset?" Angie asks. "You made out with Clark Kent. He's freaking hot."

I laugh. "Yes. He's attractive, but I guess I'm confused. What do you think Jake wants?"

She rolls her eyes. "Who cares what he wants. He probably noticed the intense attraction between you and Alexander that day we saw him at lunch. I'm sure he's jealous."

"Forget about him. He abandoned you when you were on a vacation with him," Gina exclaims. "He ended things, so now he has to live with his stupid mistake. Serves him right."

"I agree," Angie says as they toast their glasses.

Could that be it? Is he jealous? He only saw us for a few minutes. I don't think we acted like there was anything going on between us.

"I doubt he's jealous," I say. "We were just having lunch when we saw him. It's not like we were on a date."

Angie folds her arms. "Don't underestimate him. Guys can be just as jealous and catty as women. The question is, would you really give him another chance if he asked?"

Both Angie and Gina are looking at me, waiting for my answer. But I don't have an answer because I don't know. I was so hurt when he ended things, but there is a part of me that still has feelings for him. You just don't stop loving a person because they hurt you.

"Let's decide on our costumes," I say, changing the subject.

Thankfully, that is the perfect distraction. I know I won't be able to avoid Jake forever, but making him wait is nothing compared to what he put me through this summer.

"Let's go with the Disney Villains—Cruella de Vil and Evil Queen," I say finally.

Angie claps. "Finally."

Both Angie and Gina leave after brunch. The café is right near a small park, so I decide to take a walk since I have the day off. There has always been something magical about this time of year. I notice the leaves changing, the smells, even people seem to act differently. I sit down on a bench and take it all in for a few minutes. I know I need to call Jake, and even though he's the one who wanted this breakup, I'm really nervous to talk to him. I'm assuming he's finally ready to give me the real explanation, so I plan on being honest with him and tell him how much he hurt me. I don't know what's going to happen with Alexander but maybe that's okay. Maybe I can just enjoy being single and my friends and my job. I take my phone out of my bag and scroll through my messages until I find Jake's. I finally send him my reply:

Okay. I will meet you. When?

A few seconds later, my phone rings. Jake is calling me.

I take a few deep breaths.

"Hello."

"Hi, Summer. I just wanted to thank you for agreeing to meet me."

Ugh. This is almost as awkward as seeing him in person, but somehow I muster up a huge dose of courage.

"That's fine. I will be home this afternoon if you want to stop by." I'm not planning on putting a lot of effort into this, so I will make him come to me.

"That sounds good. How about this evening? I can bring something from Antonio's."

My heart sinks. What's he trying to do, twist the knife even further? Antonio's was one of our favorite takeout spots.

"Um . . . don't worry about it. Just come by anytime," I reply.

After I hang up, I'm practically shaking. It's done. Jake and I are meeting tonight. *It's going to be okay*, I tell myself. I need to get this closure in order to move on with my life. I enjoy the park for a few minutes, and then I head home. I hope this isn't a mistake.

There's a knock at my door, and I close my eyes and take a few breaths. I've spent most of the afternoon trying to mentally prepare myself to talk to Jake. Except when I answer the door it's not Jake, it's Mrs. Rothera.

"Hi," I say, trying to hide my surprise. She looks very concerned.

"I'm sorry to bother you. I was just making sure you were okay."

I have an uneasy feeling. What does she mean by that?

"I'm fine."

She still doesn't look convinced, and now she's starting to scare me. I guess I should just tell her about Jake coming over.

"Okay, fine. Jake sent me a message last week about wanting to talk. He should be here any minute."

I bite my lip and wait for her chime in. I'm sure she has something to say, and I kind of want to know what it is, but she doesn't say a word.

"Okay, I give in—am I making a mistake?" I plead as I grab ahold of her arms.

She stares into my eyes. "Well, that all depends on what you want to come out of this meeting."

That's not the answer I was expecting from her. I turn around, leaving her in the doorway.

"I want closure," I say as I fall down on the couch. "I want to know why he ended things so abruptly with no warning." I cover my eyes with my arm. "We were on vacation, enjoying our time together, and he just left."

She closes the door and joins me in the living room. "You will get your answer. As long as you ask for the right reason."

What is she saying? Why is she talking in code? Just then, there's another knock at the door.

Mrs. Rothera looks at me and puts her hand on my arm. "Sometimes things aren't what they seem."

There she goes again. I want to ask her what she means, but Jake knocks a second time. I go to the door to answer it.

"Hey," he says with a nervous smile. When he sees Mrs. Rothera, his smile fades.

"I was just leaving. Have a good night." She hurries out the door.

My heart is beating so fast. I look at Jake who shoves his hands in his pockets as he rocks back and forth on his heels.

"Thanks for letting me come over," he says as he walks in and looks around the room. I wonder if he's thinking about all the time we spent here together. I hope he is, and I hope the guilt starts eating away at him. I still live here and I'm reminded of it every day.

"It's fine," I reply. I'm waiting for him to start talking because this was his idea.

"Why was Mrs. Rothera here?" he asks.

I walk past him and sit down on the couch. "She wanted to check in on me. We've kind of become . . . friends." I guess that's what you could call us . . . or something like that.

Jake walks over and sits across from me. "There's something strange about her." He pauses. "When I dropped the key off to her, she kept asking me if I thought about what I was doing. I didn't give her any information about what had happened but it was like she already knew."

Hah. This still doesn't prove anything. He was giving her his key and it doesn't take a genius to figure out that we had broken up.

"I'm sure it wasn't too hard for her to figure out," I say coldly. "Giving her your key when you could have left it with me. That's kind of obvious."

He hangs his head. "I know. I just couldn't face you. I didn't know what else to do and it just seemed like the easiest thing."

I fold my arms defensively. "Easy? So you just wanted the easy way out after almost two years together."

I surprise myself with the way I just blurted that out, but I may as well get to the point.

He frowns. "I definitely deserve that . . . which is why I'm here." He pauses. "After seeing you and Angie the other day, I haven't been able to stop thinking about everything that happened."

Hmm . . . maybe Angie was right and seeing Alexander influenced his decision.

I purse my lips. "Okay."

"I freaked out," he exclaims. "I mean, come on—we were on vacation together. I just wasn't ready to get engaged."

Engaged? What the hell is he talking about?

"All those girls talking about rings and weddings just got to me. Especially when they said that we were going to be first to get married."

I jump up from the couch. "What are you talking about?"

He gives me a blank stare. "Angie, Lauren, and Shelby were sitting out on the deck planning our wedding before we were even engaged," he exclaims.

I don't believe this. He broke up with me because he overheard a conversation. This has to be a joke. I consider throwing him out, but then I remember what Mrs. Rothera said about things not being what they seem.

I rub my forehead. "So you threw away our relationship based on a conversation you overheard, is that what you're telling me? You didn't even think of discussing it with me. You just up and left."

He stares at the floor. "I guess," he whispers. "When I got back, I felt so bad that I came here to get my stuff. I gave Mrs. Rothera the key, and I just threw myself into work. I realized pretty quickly that I made a huge mistake, but I assumed it was too late."

I don't look at him as he gives me his explanation. "It wasn't until I saw you that day at lunch that I realized I had to see you again, at least to tell you how sorry I am."

I can feel the tears coming but I hold them back. I finally look at him.

"Well, you've seen me," I snap. "You can leave now."

His face falls. "I'll leave, but can I just ask one thing?"

I glare at him. "What?"

"Would you consider just taking some time to think about everything? I'm not going to ask you to give me another chance, yet. But, if there's a chance you still love me . . ."

I get up and walk to the door. I pull it open, waiting for him to walk out. "Good night, Jake."

He frowns but he doesn't try to argue.

"I still love you," he says before he walks out.

I shut the door behind him and fall to the ground. The tears that I was holding in finally make their way down my face. So much for a fresh new start. I feel like I'm back on the beach the night he left me in tears.

Chapter Seven

*W*hen I arrive at the house, Melanie's car is parked out front. I haven't seen her since she walked in on Alexander and me kissing. I already gave myself a pep talk to keep my cool and be as professional as possible. Not to mention I'm really tired. I didn't get much sleep after seeing Jake last night and I'm really not in the mood for Melanie's attitude.

I quietly walk into the house, which is completely ridiculous because there is no way I can avoid her.

"Good morning, Summer," she calls warmly. I stop in my tracks. That's Melanie's voice but she sounds different, almost happy. I follow her voice into the living room.

She's sitting on the couch surrounded by stacks of papers. She looks up when I walk in. "How are you?" she says cheerfully. Admittedly, I don't know what to say.

"Hi. I'm fine," I say slowly. She's humming softly to herself. I feel really stupid just lingering in the doorway. "Um—the electrician should be here soon to switch out the lighting fixtures in the kitchen. Can you let me know when they arrive? I'll be in the office."

She nods. "Okay."

I walk toward Alexander's office. Maybe the little talk Alexander had with her did some good. Regardless, I'll take it. I don't have the energy to put forth a ton of effort with her today. I sit down at the desk and pull out my planner. I'm trying to work but I can't concentrate. And it's not just because of what happened with Jake last night. Melanie's behavior has completely thrown me off guard.

"Are you ready for the party?" I look up to see her standing in the doorway. I hate to be so negative but I don't trust this woman.

"We're getting there," I reply. I scroll through my emails in order to make it look like I'm busy (which I'm not). My efforts fail because she comes in and sits down across the desk from me. I look up from my screen to see her staring at me. I hate feeling like I'm being watched.

"Did you need something?" I ask her politely as I lean back in the chair.

She gives me a smug smile. "No. I just wanted to tell you not to worry about me walking in the other night." I shift around uncomfortably in my seat. I guess it's good that she's putting it out there so it's not the elephant in the room.

"Oh. Well, thanks." That sounded really stupid, but I don't know what else to say. Mostly because I'm not worried about what she thinks other than I prefer to not have to work in a hostile environment. She's still looking at me, and I'm growing more and more uncomfortable.

"Melanie, I don't want things to be awkward between us. I know you've worked with Alexander a long time."

"Yes, I have," she interrupts. "And that's why I'm telling you not to worry about it. This isn't the first time this has happened."

Okay. What is that supposed to mean?

"This isn't the first time what has happened?" I ask. I can feel my blood pressure creeping up.

She gives a fake laugh. "Come on. Let's be honest, Alexander has a lot going for him. Do you really think you're the first woman to come around here and mesmerize him?"

I raise my eyebrows. This girl has issues, either she's trying to antagonize me or she's trying to make herself feel better. Either way, I need to keep my cool.

"I don't think I mesmerize him," I say flatly. "We enjoy each other's company and we have a lot in common." I try to focus my attention back on my computer screen. I can see out of the corner of my eye that her smile has faded to a glare.

"Think what you want, but as soon as you finish this job, you will be gone—just like the rest of them."

Hmmm . . . the rest of them? I know what she's trying to do and I'm not going to let her get to me.

"I'm going to do what I was hired to do. And if I make a new friend in the process that's great."

She rolls her eyes. "Anyway, I'll let you get back to work." She practically dances out of the office.

I clench my fists. *Don't let her get you upset*, I think to myself. I know she's trying to convince herself that there's nothing between Alexander and me. And maybe there isn't other than a physical attraction. Either way, this is my career.

I somehow make it through the rest of the day without any more run-ins with Melanie. Luckily, I'm busy with the electrician and doing different tasks around the house. And she's busy with whatever it is that she does for Alexander all day. It's not until right before I leave that she speaks to me again.

"Alexander gave me a list of a few things to do for the party, including inviting some of his friends. He said I needed to contact your friend Angie."

I smile. This is actually a good thing. I would love to see her try to interact with Angie.

"Yep. Angie is the one planning this party. I don't really have anything to do with it."

She glances at her phone. "Angie may be doing the planning, but being that the party is here, I will be handling things for Alexander *of course*."

I want to remind her that as his assistant she works for him just like me, that she's not his girlfriend or his wife. And I really want to tell her that the way she falls all over him is pathetic. However, I bite my tongue (I seem to be doing this a lot).

I scroll through my phone and forward her Angie's contact information. "I just sent you her info. Give her a call."

I leave for the day before I say anything that could get me fired. I'm just going to ignore her comment about Alexander and the other women. Or at least I'm going to try to.

I'm really trying to ignore everything Melanie said but it's proving to be really hard. She's totally succeeding in getting under my skin, which is exactly what she wanted. Over the next week, whenever Alexander is around so is Melanie. It could be just me but I notice that he's very careful around her. It's almost as if he's trying to spare her feelings so he's been keeping his distance.

We are one week out from the party and I'm busy hanging garland on the banister when Alexander joins me on the stairs.

"Everything looks great," he says. "Are you excited for the party?"

I nod. "Yeah. How about you?"

He nods. I can tell he's about to say something else.

"Summer . . ." He hesitates. "I owe you an apology."

I give him a curious look. "For what?"

He scratches his neck. "Because I've been so out of it lately. I don't want you to get the wrong idea."

I lay the garland down and sit down on the step below him.

"The wrong idea? What do you mean?"

I don't like the sound of this. Maybe Melanie got to him after all.

"I don't want you to think that me being distracted has anything to do with you. Things at work haven't been great."

I give him a sympathetic look. "I'm sorry to hear that."

He takes a deep breath. "I did want to ask you something, though. I was wondering if you were going to the party with anyone?"

I smile. "Going with anyone—as in a date? No. I just figured Angie would put me to work when I got here."

He laughs. "Probably."

I bite my lip, waiting for him to say something else. I'm not sure if he's going to ask me to be his date or not. Or maybe he's checking to see if I'm going with someone else.

"I was going to ask if you want to go together, but I just realized that sounds pretty stupid considering it's at my house and we were both going to be here anyway."

I start to giggle. "I'm sorry for laughing," I say. He starts laughing, too. "But, to answer your question, I would love to go to your party with you. We can just meet here," I say, trying to keep a straight face.

He doesn't say anything. Instead, he leans down and kisses me. And it's just like I remembered. It's a good thing I'm sitting down because my legs feel weak. When we pull away, I look around to see if Melanie is watching from anywhere. I think it's finally time to address the situation with her.

"I actually wanted to talk to you about something," I say as I look around again. "In private, if possible."

He gives me a concerned look but follows me up the stairs into one of the guest rooms. He sits down on the bench at the end of the bed.

"What's wrong?" he asks immediately.

I sigh. "I just wanted to talk to you about Melanie."

His smile quickly fades. "I told you I spoke to her. Everything is fine."

I sigh. "Actually, I don't think it is."

Not a second later, there is a knock on the door, which is ajar. Sure enough, it's Melanie. I roll my eyes.

"I'm so sorry to interrupt," she says innocently. "Edward has been calling you nonstop. He just called my phone looking for you."

Alexander groans. "Of course he is. Summer, can we continue this later?"

"Yes, definitely."

He leaves to go call Edward back (I have no idea who Edward is). I automatically think of Edward Cullen from *Twilight* when I hear that name.

Melanie is lingering in the doorway. I walk toward the door when she stands in front of me.

"Is everything all right?"

I give her a fake smile. "Everything is great. Just making plans for the party."

She glares at me as I nonchalantly walk past her. I go back to hanging the garland, and she silently walks past me down the stairs. I think it's safe to assume that we've officially drawn a line in the sand, and if there is any possibility of a future with Alexander, I need to address this with him.

Chapter Eight

I officially hate my costume. I told Angie that I didn't care which villain I was so she took the Cruella de Vil costume. I'm dressed as the Evil Queen from *Snow White* and I'm sweating like a pig. Although this costume could look good on some people, I'm not one of those people. So much for looking cute and sexy on the first holiday I'm single. I guess, technically, I'm Alexander's date for the evening, but I'm still very single.

Unfortunately, I still haven't had a chance to talk to him about Melanie. Every time I saw him this week Melanie was right there (shocker). Speaking of this, the house looks amazing. I'm almost finished decorating the entire downstairs with the exception of a guest room and bathroom, and Angie and I spent the whole day yesterday setting up for the party.

I stand in front of the full-length mirror looking at this hideous costume. I guess I can't blame Jake for wanting to wear a T-shirt last year because that actually sounds awesome right now.

I hear a knocking at my door, and I make a face in the mirror. I really don't want to answer the door looking like this, much less go out in public. When I answer the door, I find Mrs. Rothera dressed in her psychic costume . . . or is it a uniform? Maybe psychics have to wear a uniform, too.

"That's a very nice costume," she says kindly.

I frown. "Thanks for being nice but you can admit it's awful."

She smiles. "I'm on my way to meet your friend Angie. I just wanted to check on you."

Why does she keep checking on me? I'm starting to get a complex that something is always going wrong.

"Everything is great. It's Halloween," I insist.

She nods slowly. "All Hallows' Eve—the most mysterious night of the year. A lot can happen tonight." I stop fidgeting with my costume. "Is that your way of telling me to expect something to happen tonight?"

She looks around my apartment. I wonder if she's looking for something. "Let's just say I have a strong feeling that tonight is going to be very eventful," she says softly.

Crap. Nothing like freaking me out before the evening even starts. "Eventful as in good or eventful as in bad?" I ask.

She gives me a weak smile. "I'm not exactly sure. Everything is kind of blurry."

Blurry? This is just great, Angie hired a psychic who can't see anything.

"Why is it blurry? Are you saying you can't see anything?"

She places her hand on my arm. "I didn't say that. I see a lot of things, but for some reason, this isn't clear." She's waving her hand around me. "I need to go get set up. I'm glad everything is okay here." She walks toward the door and I follow her.

Well, it was okay before she came and made me worry. Figures. She drops a hint like that and then has to leave. "I guess I will see you later," I say.

She nods. "Yes."

After she leaves, I'm really nervous. I wish I knew what to expect tonight. I run through every possible scenario in my head. Maybe it has something to do with me and Alexander or maybe me and Melanie. What if something happens to Alexander's house? Angie did say that she was expecting a hundred people. I suddenly feel sick to my stomach. I'm not sure if it's nerves or that I'm overheated under this disgusting polyester dress and headpiece. I try to calm myself down, so I take off my costume and hang it in the garment bag. I will just change when I get over there so I don't have to drive in the stupid thing. I load up my car and make my way to Alexander's. I guess it wouldn't be Halloween without some excitement.

"Why aren't you dressed?" Angie yells as soon as she sees me. Of course she looks great in her costume. I really should have paid more attention to the costume selection. I was too distracted with that stupid Jake.

"Relax," I say, holding up the garment bag. "I was about to pass out in the thing, so I figured I would change here." Angie scowls and walks off in a huff. I can't believe she's mad at me about this, although, maybe that's what Mrs. Rothera was referring to. Maybe this is part of the eventful evening she couldn't see.

In order to put off changing into my costume, I decide to wander around and check on the party; after all, I am supposed to be helping. The house looks fantastic, and I'm not just talking about my decorating. The fall/Halloween décor makes it look and feel so festive. In the kitchen, there are trays of catered food everywhere and it all smells divine. I recognize Angie's cousin, Vinny (a bartender) and her boyfriend Brett setting up a full bar in the corner of Alexander's game room. Vinny is dressed as a prisoner and Brett is dressed (or sort of dressed) as a Chippendales dancer. My eyes grow wide and I quickly cover my mouth to hide my shock. He looks as scary as ever.

When I walk past the French doors that lead out to the lanai, I notice a tent set up with a sign that says, "Psychic Readings." I have to admit it does give a fun Halloween-like feel to the party despite the butterflies I feel in my stomach.

"Summer, I promise I'm not mad at you but please go get dressed before the guests start to arrive," Angie says, interrupting my thought. She has her hands in prayer position.

"Fine," I say, rolling my eyes. "By the way, have you seen Alexander?"

Her exasperated look turns into a wicked smile. "Oh yeah, and he looks good."

"Shhh," I shriek, pulling her outside on the lanai. "Don't forget a lot of his friends will be here, so please don't say anything to embarrass me." She looks shocked that I'd ever suggest such a thing. "Oh, come on, don't act like it's not a possibility. Anyway, do you know where he is?"

She shrugs. "I'm not sure, but he was asking about you," she says in a singsong voice. I can feel myself start to blush as she continues talking. "That doesn't matter now, you can chase after him later—go get changed," she says as she starts to drag me back into the house. Just then, Mrs. Rothera pops out of her tent, startling me.

"Oh, you scared me," I exclaim.

"Sorry," she says as she fixes her sign. Angie heads inside but not before giving me a stern look. She's acting like my mom.

I stand awkwardly with Mrs. Rothera. "I met your friend Alexander a little while ago. He's very handsome."

I'm not sure if she's telling me this to make conversation or if there is another reason. I've realized I've become extremely paranoid over everything she says.

"Yes," I agree. "Well, I suppose I need to get changed before Angie has a meltdown. Um, good luck tonight," I say. I don't know if that's the appropriate thing to say to a psychic. It's kind of like telling her not to screw up anyone's idea of his or her future. I walk inside and pick up my costume from the bench I dropped it on and head to the guest room to change. Alexander's office just happens to be on the way, and sure enough, he's sitting at his desk with his hair slicked back, wearing a black leather jacket. I should have known he would dress as a T-Bird. I sigh. I should have gone with Angie's first suggestion and worn a Pink Ladies costume.

"Nice costume," I say playfully. He looks up from his laptop and smiles. "Hi. And thank you." He pauses, eyeing me curiously. "And where is your costume? I thought Halloween was your day."

I hold up the garment bag. "It's in here and it's absolutely horrible. I look like a nun, and the headpiece is so tight around my face I feel like it cuts off my circulation."

He laughs. "I'm sure you look very cute."

I roll my eyes. "Don't hold your breath."

He stands up and walks around to the front of his desk to where I'm standing. He puts his arms around my waist and pulls me close to him. I admit I'm taken aback a little. I can smell the leather of his jacket.

"I think you're gorgeous," he says softly. "And I'm sure you look great even in a horrible nun costume."

He pulls me even closer and clasps his hands together behind my back.

"Well, it's actually the Evil Queen from *Snow White*," I whisper.

He doesn't say another word as he leans in and kisses me. This kiss is more intense than last week when we were sitting on the stairs. In between kisses, I drag my lips away from his. "The party will be starting soon."

"Mmmhmm," he mumbles.

I pull away again. "You have to promise me you won't avoid me like the plague when you see me in my costume."

He laughs. "I promise."

I sigh. "Okay, here I go. I'll see you out there," I say, giving him one more kiss. I pick up my costume from where I dropped it.

"Can't wait," he exclaims.

As soon as I turn the corner out of his office (and out of his sight), I jump up and down excitedly. If the last few minutes are any indication of what Mrs. Rothera was thinking would happen, then it's going to be an awesome evening.

Chapter Nine

"It doesn't look *that* bad," Gina says. She has to be the worst liar on the planet. And it's easy for her to say being that she's dressed in lingerie. She says she's dressed as a sexy cat but really it's just lingerie and a pair of cat ears.

"Thanks, but you're lying," I reply, taking a long sip of my wine. I'm going to need a lot of wine tonight to hide my embarrassment. I've been looking around for Alexander but I haven't been able to talk to him since our little make out session in his office.

The party is a huge success so far, and there is a line outside Mrs. Rothera's tent. I guess I'm the only one who's a chicken when it comes to knowing what my future holds.

"Where is he?" Gina asks, looking around. I know she's referring to Alexander.

"He's around here somewhere. I just, um . . . saw him in his office." I can feel myself blushing. Of course it could be that it's about one hundred degrees under this costume. "He may be hiding from me after having seen me in this."

All of a sudden I notice Angie rushing toward us, and she looks worried.

"What's wrong?" I ask.

She fans herself with her hands. "So, do you remember when we went to lunch with Alexander and we ran into Jake?"

My heart sinks. "Yeah."

She cringes. "And do you remember when Alexander invited Jake to come tonight?"

"Yeah. Don't tell me . . ."

She nods. "Yep, Jake's here. He actually showed his face here. I was so shocked to see him that I didn't even say anything. I just came to find you."

"Are you serious?" Gina chimes in. "I told you I should have made that call."

I can't even think straight. "She was right," I say.

Gina and Angie look confused. "Mrs. Rothera. She told me tonight was going to be eventful. Now my ex-boyfriend and my . . . um, and Alexander are both here."

Just then, Jake walks into the kitchen and looks right at me. He's actually wearing a costume; he never wanted to dress up while we were together. I'm not going to lie—my heart rate speeds up when I see him. I know I shouldn't be surprised. I was in love with Jake and those feelings don't just go away overnight, even after he explained why he broke up with me.

"Who do you think you are showing up here?" Gina shouts across the room. The other guests who are milling around turn to look at her.

"Gina, stop," Angie demands.

Jake calmly walks toward us. "Not that it's any of your business, Gina, but I was invited." I'm completely silent.

"Yeah, well, Alexander didn't know who you were when he invited you," Angie says, raising her voice.

"Okay, guys, I will handle this," I interrupt before a brawl breaks out and before Gina makes a phone call. "Jake, let's go outside and talk," I say, walking toward the front door. He follows me outside.

"Look, Summer, I know this might have been a mistake, but I needed to see you," he pleads. I stand with my arms tightly folded over my chest. Again, I'm wishing I wasn't wearing this stupid costume.

"I wish you wouldn't have come," I say softly. "I met someone else Jake and I really like him."

His face falls. "So, you're saying you don't have any feelings for me anymore?"

I bite my bottom lip. What am I supposed to say? Of course I have feelings for you but you broke my heart.

"I don't know," I say calmly. "But, I do know that I like spending time with Alexander."

He nods. "Okay, I understand but just think about it, okay? I know I messed up but I'm not ready to give us up yet." He leans over and kisses me gently on the cheek. I close my eyes as the familiar scent of his cologne floods back and so do the memories.

"You were very ready to give us up this summer," I snap.

He hangs his head. "I explained that to you already."

I look away. "Just go, Jake."

He doesn't argue, and without another word, he walks away leaving me standing in the middle of Alexander's pristine manicured lawn. I touch the tips of my fingers to my cheek where he kissed me. I want to cry because I'm so confused. I meant what I said about Alexander, I really like him—a lot. I guess this proves that I should have gone with my gut and never gotten involved with him. I don't know if I'm ready yet.

Suddenly, a light bulb goes on in my head and I know what I need to do. I head back into the house and make my way toward Mrs. Rothera's tent. As I walk through the living room, Melanie jumps in front of me. She's dressed as Wonder Woman. "Having fun, Summer? Nice costume by the way." She gives me a wicked smile.

I groan. "Thanks. And, yes, I'm having a good time, but if you'll excuse me, I have to do something."

She ignores me. "It's a great party, kudos to your friend Angie. Too bad you've been too preoccupied to enjoy it."

I feel sick to my stomach. "I don't know what you're talking about."

She cocks her head to the side. "Oh, sure you do." Crap! She must have seen me talking to Jake. Was she watching me the entire time?

"I don't have to explain anything to you because it's none of your business," I say as I start to walk away. She grabs my elbow. I look down at her hand and yank my elbow away from her grasp.

"That's where you're wrong. It is my job to look out for Alexander's best interest, and it's very clear that you're playing him."

We're standing in the middle of the room ready to face off when I notice Alexander and Angie watching us. My eyes meet Alexander's and I can tell he's not happy. I decide to be the better person and not respond to Melanie's accusation. Angie quickly walks toward us and asks to speak to me in private.

"What has gotten in to you tonight?" she demands. "First you disappear with Jake and now you're arguing with Alexander's assistant. Did Jake leave or do I need to have him escorted out?"

I don't want to explain anything to Angie. I want to talk to Mrs. Rothera and try to figure out what's going on in my head.

"He's gone," I say softly.

She gets a big smile on her face. "Good for you. I was hoping you would tell him to get lost. I still can't believe he showed up."

I look down and remember I'm still in this horrible costume. Maybe I should just change, because I'm not enjoying this party at all.

"Ang, I need to take care of something," I say, ignoring her comments about Jake.

Thankfully she doesn't question me. I rush out to Mrs. Rothera's tent, and she emerges from her tent as soon as I approach.

"I'm ready to talk," I say boldly. She nods and holds the side of the tent open. It almost seems as if she knew I was coming. When I sit down on the stool inside, I look around. I notice a few books and crystals on the table. She sits down across from me.

"I just wanted to say I'm sorry," I say immediately. "I shouldn't have been so cold toward you. I was just surprised about all of this," I say, waving my arms.

She shrugs. "I know. It can be overwhelming, and I was pressuring you to get a reading because I wanted to help you. After you returned from your vacation, I could feel the pain you were going through. Your aura is strong and you usually give off a very positive vibe. But when you came home, you were dark and distant . . . that is until you became involved with this man." She points toward the house. I know she's talking about Alexander.

She closes her eyes and takes a few deep breaths before she starts talking. "You're confused and you want to know if you should give Jake another chance. You still have feelings for him."

I let out a frustrated sigh. "Yep."

"You shouldn't feel guilty about this," she says as she reaches over and takes my hands in hers.

I do feel guilty—guilty and confused.

"Yes, I still have feelings for Jake, but I'm also very drawn to Alexander," I whine. She leans in and looks me directly in my eyes. Of course it feels like she's looking through me again.

"There was a reason that you were meant to come here," she says firmly. "Both you and Alexander were searching for something. He was searching for a fresh start and you were searching for a distraction."

I think about the timing of everything. I received the message from Melanie right after Jake ended things. Were Alexander and I meant to find each other at just the right time? Then I remember what she told me the last time we talked about him.

"The last time we talked about this you mentioned there was another woman involved. Is that something I should be concerned about?"

I remember what Alexander told me about seeing his ex-wife, a.k.a. the hot Swedish model. Every time I think about her I cringe. I can only imagine what her Halloween costume looks like.

"There is another woman, but the connection you and Alexander have is strong, almost magical," she says firmly. "You should go talk to him now."

All of a sudden it hits that I haven't seen him all night other than in his office. After my altercation with Melanie, I rushed out to see Mrs. Rothera. He looked very upset and I ran off.

"Melanie!" I scream. "It's her; she's the other woman."

I jump up from the stool and rush out of the tent, running into a line of people waiting for their own time with the

Halloween psychic. I tear through the house, passing Gina who's doing shots. *Seriously? Are we at a frat party?*

I rush from room to room searching for Alexander. I don't see him, so I make my way to his office. The door is closed but I barge in. Sure enough, he's standing at the window looking out over the lawn. He looks at me and then turns back toward the window. It's obvious that I'm too late. Melanie already got to him.

"Alexander. I'm so sorry," I apologize.

He turns around and walks toward me.

"Summer, you don't have anything to apologize for. I'm happy for you."

What? I open my mouth to say something, but he continues talking. "I should have never pursued you, especially after you told me about your recent breakup. I tried to keep my distance as much as possible. I even stayed in the city when I knew you would be here because I knew if I were here I would want to spend time with you and get to know you better. Honestly, I didn't intend to have you decorate my whole house until . . . well, until I met you. I was drawn to you."

My mouth is hanging open as I listen to him unload is feelings. "I guess I only have myself to blame. I did invite your ex-boyfriend to come tonight."

Something comes over me and I'm not sure what it is. Maybe it's the memory of when Jake left me at the beach or maybe it's the feeling I have when I'm here. I think about the many days I didn't want to go home to my lonely apartment that's full of memories of the past.

"Jake and I are not back together," I blurt out. He looks confused, so I explain. "I'm not going to lie and tell you that I don't still care about him, it's probably too soon for that. But, I really like being here and being with you. I want to get to know you better, if that's something you still want."

He sits down on one of the chaise lounges, so I do the same.

"I'm confused. Melanie said you were outside with Jake and things were . . . intense. And then I saw you and her arguing before you ran off."

I look down at the ground. "I know—I've wanted to talk to you about Melanie but we haven't had much of a chance to be alone, and when we are together, we . . ."

The corner of his mouth curls up. I'm sure he's thinking the same thing as me.

"Melanie hates me, and she doesn't want me anywhere near you," I tell him. "She's counting down the days for this job to be finished. I know how important she is to you so I would never ask you to choose."

He sighs. "She's very protective of me. I know there may be

deeper feelings there, but I've told her there would never be anything more between her and me."

Alexander and I sit quietly. I look down at my hideous costume and remember that I'm supposed to be enjoying a Halloween party right now. This entire night has been a nightmare, and I'm sure Angie is really mad at me.

"I should check in with Angie. I will let you think," I say, breaking our silence. I stand up and make my way toward the door.

"Wait," he exclaims. I turn around and Alexander walks toward me. He takes my face in his hands and kisses me. I wrap my arms tightly around his neck, and his hands move from my face to around my waist.

When he stops kissing me, he touches his forehead to mine. "The first day we met, right here in this office, I knew you were meant to come into my life. The time I spend with you is . . . it's like magic." *Wow. That's what Mrs. Rothera just said.*

"I want to see where this can go, more than anything, but I don't want to rush you. We could continue to take things slow," he continues.

I run my hands down his arms. "I would really like that."

He smiles. "There is one thing, though—tonight doesn't count as our first date."

I laugh. "Please no. It has been very eventful, though, but I guess it wouldn't be Halloween without some craziness."

I know I still need to address the issue of Melanie and her hatred of me.

"What about Melanie?" I ask. "I really made the effort to get along with her in the beginning. I finally just gave up."

He scratches his head. "I will sit down and have a talk with her. She's my assistant, and she does an excellent job. However, she needs to stay out of my personal life."

I feel a sense of relief come over me. Without saying a word, Alexander takes my hand in his and leads me back to the party. Of course, Angie gives me a dirty look as soon as she sees me. However, her dirty look fades when she notices Alexander's hand tightly holding on to mine. She raises her eyebrows but tries to hide her curiosity. Hopefully she will recognize my happiness and forgive me for ditching her on our holiday.

Chapter Ten

*W*hat a night. Surprisingly, I enjoy the remainder of the party despite all the chaos that ensued earlier. I spend a good ten minutes talking to Gina, trying to convince her *not* to make any phone calls to her family members. She can't seem to get over Jake showing up. Of course I'd rather not talk about Jake because I've made my decision and I know I'm ready to move on with my life.

Angie finally breaks her silent treatment to me after I practically have to get on my hands and knees asking for forgiveness. According to her, I broke the cardinal rule of our holiday, which is paying more attention to a man than us celebrating together. She also made me take a bunch of pictures in our costumes. I'm planning on blocking all those photos from all of my social media sites.

Alexander happily introduced me to all of his friends. I even meet a few people who are interested in a new interior decorator. I never thought about it but having this party at his house is a great way to show my talents. I guess I owe Angie a big thank you for harassing me with all those calls that day I was here with Alexander. I wish I had a picture of Melanie's face when she saw Alexander and me hand in hand. At least she knows that her big plan backfired.

While Alexander is talking, I glance out toward Mrs. Rothera's tent and, sure enough, she's watching me intently. I excuse myself and make my way over to her.

She gives me a wave and a smug look. "Hi, looks like you're enjoying yourself."

She's acting like she's surprised but I know she isn't. "Now I am." I pause. "It's been quite an eventful night, just like you said it would be."

She gives me an innocent smile.

"Anyway, I just wanted to thank you for being so kind to me over the past few weeks, for constantly checking in on me, and for bringing me that yummy soup. It was much better than a Lean Cuisine meal. I really appreciate your friendship."

She laughs. "I'm glad I could help." She points to where Alexander is still standing. "I take it everything is working out."

I shrug my shoulders. "We're taking things slow. He knows I'm still getting over a broken heart."

She pats me on the shoulder. "Good."

A part of me wants to ask her what's going to happen with Alexander and me. But when I look over at him, I feel an overwhelming sense of excitement. Maybe it's better that I don't know what's going to happen. I look back at Mrs. Rothera and suddenly she has a very concerned look on her face.

"What is it?" I ask worriedly.

She scrunches her face. "I just . . . if I can offer you one more piece of advice."

I nod quickly. "Of course."

"Be honest with him and *demand* the same in return."

I stare at her blankly. "Okay."

Alexander joins us, and she gives him a warm smile. "Are you ready for your turn?" she asks him.

He starts laughing. "No. I think I'm good." He takes my hand in his. "I don't need to know what my future holds. I'm very content with where I am right now."

I can feel my face get red again. This time I know it's not the costume.

The party rages on until the wee hours of the morning. Okay, so maybe it doesn't rage on, but it does go really late and everyone seems to be having an awesome time.

"Another Halloween under our belts," Angie says in between her yawns. "I guess tonight turned out okay after all. It certainly looks like it did for you anyway."

I hit her on her arm. "It was a great night. Your party was a huge success."

She raises her eyebrows. "Are you going to give me details of your night or do I need to ask Alexander?"

I giggle. "The only details you need to know are that Alexander and I are taking things slowly and that for the first time in a while I'm really happy."

She gives me a hug. "I'm happy for you." When she pulls away, she grabs my arms tightly. "Does that mean Jake is finally out of the picture?"

I nod. "Yeah. I'm ready to move on."

Angie starts clapping. "So, since this party was such a smashing success, let's talk about Christmas."

I hold my hands up. "Uh-uh, you're on your own for that one. I'll help you with decorations but that's it."

She giggles. "I was hoping you would say that. I'm sure I will be in need of some of your decorating magic."

Surprisingly, I don't cringe when she says that. Moving on from the past also means accepting it.

"That's a deal," I say happily.

When I arrive home, I look around my apartment. For some reason it doesn't seem as lonely as it did before. I think I've come a long way in a short amount of time. The only thing that has me curious is Mrs. Rothera's advice, but like I told her, I don't need to know what my future holds. For now, I'm going to enjoy my life and take things as they come. I have high hopes for my relationship with Alexander as long as the issue with Melanie gets under control. After all of tonight's drama was over, I made some good business contacts thanks to Alexander. I already have three potential new clients and I'm ready to use my decorating magic to the fullest. I've decided I shouldn't try to shy away from that phrase or my past. If there is anything I've learned this fall, it's that everything happens for a reason and people come into our lives for a reason. I'm ready for the next season of my life and whatever it may bring.

THE END

Winter Can Wait Now Available

Buy the second book in the Seasons of Summer series on Amazon or read with your KindleUnlimited membership!

As much as I love Connecticut, I despise the cold. Wasn't it just summertime yesterday? I wrap the large fleece blanket even more tightly around me while I look over the contract for my next project. Summer Interiors has been flourishing thanks to my amazing boyfriend, Alexander. My latest project is his friend Nick's new restaurant. I've never decorated a restaurant before and I'm really excited about it. He's given me a long list of preferences, so I'm planning to work around those.

Nick is an interesting guy—very outspoken and charismatic —and this weekend we're having dinner with him and his girlfriend, Caroline. I'm looking forward to getting to know Alexander's friends better. I haven't had much interaction other than at the crazy Halloween party at Alexander's home. And let's just say that wasn't the ideal setting to make new friends.

Another job I'm working on is my landlord's apartment. Mrs. Rothera and I have an interesting relationship/friendship. I guess you could say we're friends. Anyway, a few weeks ago she asked if I would be interested in helping her decorate her place. I reluctantly agreed, and I should have gone with my gut feeling. It turns out she's one of the most high maintenance clients I've ever worked with. Our building consists of four large apartments, and her place is directly below mine so it's the exact same layout. It's a nice size, so that's not the issue—the issue is the way she questions every suggestion and move I make. Being a psychic, she views the world a little differently. Yep—a psychic. I've lived here a year and never had any idea until she sprung it on me all of a sudden a few months ago.

I gather my notes and some paint swatches and head downstairs to show her. When I approach her door, I hear strange music coming from her apartment. I press my ear to the door to get a better listen. All I can hear is the sound of tambourines and chanting. I roll my eyes—here we go.

I knock loudly on the door, and surprisingly, she answers right away. I wasn't sure she would be able to hear over that noise, but on the other hand, she probably could see me coming. She is a psychic after all.

"Come in. I was just finishing my meditation," she says softly.

I walk into the dark room. She has the blinds and curtains closed. Thankfully, she turns off the music and opens the curtains. The sunlight pours into the room—much better.

"I just wanted to drop off these swatches, and I made some notes for you to take a look at," I say as I spread everything out on the table.

"Ohhh. Very nice," she says excitedly. She takes her time looking through everything. In the meantime, I get a text from Alexander. I smile to myself.

"A message from your man?" she asks, giving me a curious look. "I'm assuming things are going well."

I blush. "Yes, they are. We're going out with some friends of his on Friday night. It will be there first time I hang out with them."

Suddenly her smile fades. "Well, don't be too disappointed after only one night with new people," she says vaguely.

What's that supposed to mean?

"Disappointed?" I repeat. "Why would I be disappointed? I'm looking forward to it."

She starts flipping through the paint swatches again. "It will just take some time."

I'm silent for a few seconds. "Mrs. Rothera, is this something I should be worried about? What, are they going to hate me or something?" I give a nervous laugh.

She puts the swatches down and folds her hands on the table. "Hate is such a strong word."

She always does this—she avoids the question and gives these vague answers. What I'm getting out of this is that Alexander's friends are not going to be receptive to me at first. And that's fine because I can deal with that. It's not like they would come between us, right?

I quickly make an excuse to leave so she doesn't start giving me any more unsolicited advice.

Ugh. Now I have two days to worry about this. I definitely didn't sign up for having my own psychic. And now it appears that I do. I think it's time I found a new place to live.

Dear Reader

I hope you enjoyed *Fall Into Magic: A Novella*. Please take a few minutes to leave a review on Amazon.

Love my books? Join my Facebook reader group. Interested in a free book? Click here.

Visit my website for updates, and stay tuned for my next book coming soon.

AuthorMelissaBaldwin.com

Buy One Way Ticket on Amazon or read with your KindleUnlimited membership!

~

Would you switch lives with someone you just met?

Sabrina Monroe, bride-to-be, and Addison Bloom, lost and looking for love, are on the run, wanting to escape to a new life. As the two strangers talk at an airport, a crazy idea unfolds—one which might provide the answers they've both been looking for.

Sabrina Monroe is poised and ready for her future as Mrs. Todd Edward Blakely. Everything seems perfect, but on the big day, suddenly she's not so sure. Her nicely mapped out life ahead of her, she finds herself in her own movie scene as the runaway bride, climbing out of the bathroom window. All she can think is *escape*.

Addison Bloom needs a life makeover. She's travelled the world to find love—and failed. On her way back from yet another friend's wedding, she's starts to feel ill at the mere thought of seeing another veil that's not hers. Should she go back to New Zealand and marry her former sweetheart, or stick it out looking for love in her new home?

While pondering if she should keep chasing fairy tales or create her own fate, Addison meets a fully made up bride, short of breath, at the airport. Sabrina. As Sabrina and

Addison talk, both can see that friendships and new love could be on the horizon if they're prepared to switch lives and walk away from everything they know.

Is there such a thing as a One Way Ticket to a new life, or will they find they're running from themselves, not just the past?

～

Also by Melissa Baldwin

COZY MYSTERY

Killer Couture: A Small-Town Cozy Mystery

Poison in Paradise: a tropical romantic mystery

Movie Scripts & Madness (The Madness and Murder Mysteries #1)

Room Service & Murder (The Madness and Murder Mysteries #2)

ROMANTIC COMEDY

Can't Hurry Christmas: A Holiday Romantic Comedy

Now That We Don't Talk: A Romantic Comedy

All the Christmas Vibes: A Holiday Romantic Comedy

Love in Overtime: A Sweet Small Town Hockey Romcom (Love on Thin Ice Multi-Author Series)

Soulmates and Slapshots: A Sweet Small Town Hockey Romcom (Love in Maple Falls Multi-Author Series)

Can We Talk?: A Romantic Comedy (Question #1)

I Think He Knows?: A Romantic Comedy (Question #2)

A Very Complicated Christmas: A Holiday Romantic Comedy

Unlucky Christmas: A Holiday Romantic Comedy

It Could Happen: A Romantic Comedy

Friends ForNever: A Romantic Comedy

One Way Ticket (written with Kate O'Keeffe)

Thanks for the Love: A Novella (Thankful #1)

Thanks for the Memories (Thankful #2)

Thanks for the Friendship (Thankful #3)

Love and Ohana Drama (Twist of Fate #1

Fate and Blind Dates (Twist of Fate #2)

Glances and Taking Chances (Twist of Fate #3)

On the Road to Love (Love in the City #1)

All You Need is Love (Love in the City #2)

From Runway to Love (Love in the City #3)

Fall Into Magic (Seasons of Summer #1)

Winter Can Wait (Seasons of Summer #2)

To Spring With Love (Seasons of Summer #3)

Return to Summer (Seasons of Summer #4)

See You Soon Broadway (Broadway #1)

See You Later Broadway (Broadway #2)

An Event to Remember (Event to Remember #1)

Wedding Haters (Event to Remember #2)

Not Quite Sheer Happiness (Event to Remember #3)

About the Author

USA Today bestselling author Melissa Baldwin always dreamed of sharing her stories with the world. She brought this vision to life, becoming an award-winning, bestselling author of over thirty romantic comedies and cozy mysteries. Melissa is also a wife, mother, new empty-nester, and travel advisor.

Her books feature charming, ambitious, and real women, whom she considers part of her tribe. Although she rarely takes a day off, when she's not writing, she enjoys quality time with her family, traveling, attempting yoga poses, and booking Disney vacations. Melissa still uses a paper planner, and her guilty pleasures include Beverly Hills 90210 reruns and General Hospital.

Connect with Melissa
authormelissabaldwin.com